For a limited time, D.N. Leo gives away
Several e-books and audiobooks in the Multiverse
Collection

VISIT THE WEBSITE AND CLAIM YOUR BOOKS
http://dnleo.com

THANK YOU FOR READING!
D.N. LEO

Synopsis

When a fairy tale ends up in a bloodbath, virtue rises.

Dinah isn't just a private investigator, she solves unthinkable mysteries in the multiverse, and has never lost a case until her best friend becomes a victim in a series of mass murders. Someone is toying with the human race and sending threats across the cosmos.

Arik, an Oxford professor in mythology, holds the key to several secrets in the multiverse. When Dinah travels to Earth to seek help from him, they discover one of the secrets he knows could make him the next victim.

As the danger increases, so does their mutual attraction. But fate might have something else in store for them in a twist of a fairy tale.

Dark Solar is an urban fantasy trilogy, full of action, magic, surprises, science and romance.

All books are available at http://dnleo.com.

  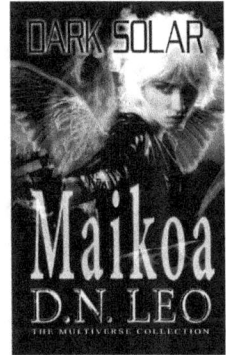

DARK SOLAR TRILOGY

http://dnleo.com

Book 1 - Oleander

Book 2 - Wolfsbane

Book 3 - Maikoa

PROLOGUE

Scotland, 1864

Jael stared at the bloodstains on what used to be the peaceful Scottish greenfield. The grass had been killed by venomous fumes, which Jael was sure were coming from Luna, the dark magic sorceress. And the bloodstains belonged to Charmine, his newly wedded wife.

The scent of Charmine mixed with her blood and the ashes from the burned bush made his hands shake, his knees weaken, his heart race with fear, and his blood boil with rage.

Jael straightened up his body. He couldn't afford a mistake right now. He couldn't let himself be weak. God had given him a second chance to live and reclaim his angel power. God wouldn't have sent him back here just to see he had failed his family. God wouldn't save his life just to let him learn he had let Charmine and their stillborn first child die at the hands of evil.

He traced his fingertips over the bloodstains. So much blood . . . but his wife was a fighter. He was sure she had survived this attack from her evil sister. *Where are you, Charmine?* His eyes desperately scanned the hillside.

He searched every inch of the vista, using every ounce of his energy along with the light source he had. He found nothing but trails of blood. Then, in the dead grass, he saw a leather-bound book covered in bloodstains. He picked it up. It was a fairy tale Charmine had just bought in town.

He had observed her from a distance as she went into the bookstore. He felt uneasy when she mixed in among humans in the middle of a crowded town. He didn't mind humans, but he disliked the supernatural creatures walking among them. The stray creatures were unpredictable, dangerous, and had a minimal sense of morality.

Jael kept at a distance to give Charmine some space. As an apprentice in the house of Gods, she rarely traveled to the outside world. Thus, whenever he had a chance, he took her on a mission with him. Earth was her favorite place in the cosmos.

When she left the busy town for the peaceful hillside, he had thought it was safe and had gone about his mission. That was one of the rare mistakes he had made in his life, and he could only hope it hadn't cost him his family. He was the angel of light with the highest ranking in his council. He was the one who gave hope to his subjects—those he had sworn to protect. Now, when he needed hope, he wasn't sure from whom he could ask it.

As the thought enraged him, he heard a noise from a large pile of charred grass. He darted over to it and yanked out a small creature. It had been wounded and burned so badly that he couldn't tell what species it was. Judging by its charred skin and what was left of its face, the creature wouldn't last long.

"What are you? Where are your people?" Jael asked without expecting a coherent answer. The creature looked like an elf. If so, it might have enough supernatural power to heal itself if he gave it some help.

He straightened the head of the creature, trying not to cause more damage to its badly damaged skin. The creature's pointy left ear moved slightly, and it opened its two eyes that glowed like two large green lightbulbs. While its ears made it look like an elf, its eyes were certainly not those of an elf.

"Take it easy. If I give you some light, like a power source, would it help? I don't want to push the light in if your body will reject it."

The creature uttered a barely audible sound. "Please," it said.

Jael nodded. He held the creature's small hands and gently pushed some light energy into its body. In a short moment, its green eyes blinked and then opened wide, looking even larger than they did before. Some of its burned patches of skin started to heal. The healthy skin began to change from a shade of orange to light green and then to a deep blue.

"You're a sea-elf!" Jael gasped. "How did you get up here? Let me take you back to the water."

"No, I'm human."

"What?"

"She made me."

"She? Do you mean Luna?"

10

The creature nodded. "She took the heart of something at sea and put it inside me . . . just to keep it beating."

"She ripped your human heart out?" Jael asked but didn't need an answer. He knew what Luna had done. It was a ritual in dark sorcery to create supernatural creatures she could control. He had always thought it was a myth. Jael asked, "Did she . . . curse someone?" and this time, he didn't wish for an answer.

The creature closed its eyes, and in a short moment, its face started to form into the shape of a young man, but as it did, its heartbeat weakened, and its breathing started to labor.

"She changed you. You're not meant to be on land. You'll die," Jael said.

"I'd rather die than live like this."

Jael said nothing. He picked the man up in his arms, spread his wings, and flew toward the water.

"You're an angel!" the man whispered.

"Yes, but I can't bring you back from death. God created you, and it's your decision to keep your life or not. But nobody has the right to take life or your heart away from you."

"If you had come earlier, you could have saved her."

Something inside him broke. It might have been his heart. Flying against the strong wind, he looked down and asked the man, "Did you see Luna kill my wife?"

"Oh . . . oh dear God, that was your wife? No, she fought hard. She didn't die. She killed Luna. And as you can see, Luna burned everything before she died."

"So why did you say I could have saved my wife if I'd come earlier?"

They had arrived at the coastline. Jael put him down close to the edge of the water. The man was weakening every second he drew in air. Jael dragged him into the water.

"Angel, what is your name?"

"I'm Jael. I am the angel of light."

"I want to die as a man."

"Not on my watch. I can't let you do that."

"Luna cursed your child before she died."

Jael stopped breathing for a second. "With what?"

"She planted the heart in me and took me to the hill. I heard her chanting a spell, and I think she wanted to place this heart into your wife's body after she cursed your child to have no heart. She was going to rip the heart out of your wife and replace it with this one . . ."

Jael stopped dragging the man to deep water. The man stood up as he had now regained some strength.

"She cursed our child?"

"Yes, I'm so sorry. Your wife killed her after that. But the curse had been completed."

"Did you see where my wife went?"

The man shook his head. "No, but she didn't go by herself. She was hurt badly. Someone took her, and I saw its shadow. Whoever or whatever it was, it was very large. I couldn't see much. I'm sorry. It might have wings . . . just like yours. But I don't think it was an angel."

"Why?"

The man looked at Jael. "Because angels don't rip someone's heart out with their bare hands. That thing took Luna's heart. Then it grabbed your wife and vanished."

Jael nodded. "You should go."

The man bowed. "I owe you my life," he said then dove into the water and swam away.

Jael looked to the horizon where the water met the sky. He swore to bring Charmine and their child home. He was an angel, and he had been protecting his subjects without fail for more than a hundred years. Now, the most important subjects in his life were in trouble. If he failed to save his own family, wouldn't it defeat the whole purpose of God creating him?

Among those at the same rank, he was the best of them all. In a hundred years of battle, he had lost only once. And that loss was to the person who had just taken Charmine.

PART ONE

CHAPTER 1

Dinah walked around the exclusive chemical lab at the headquarters of LeBlanc Pharmaceuticals in London. It had been three days, and she hadn't been able to develop the compound Ciaran had asked her to make. In Iilos, she would have blamed limited resources. She looked around and sighed. Any government in the cosmos would be drooling just to get their hands on this lab. The slow process could be because she had never before made weapons of this caliber. Or maybe she wasn't as good as she had thought and should settle for being a private investigator rather chemical engineer. But damn it, she *liked* chemistry.

Dinah frowned and rubbed her thumb on the button of the weaponry jacket Ciaran had made for her. He always asked for two-hundred percent commitment from those who worked for him. He wasn't king of the most prosperous universe in the multiverse for no reason.

A week ago, Earth time, Arete had challenged Ciaran, his council, and Arik to the second round of the multiversal hologame. Xiilok rebels had used a toxic fume that had nearly killed Ciaran and Madeline, and Ciaran believed they'd use an even more lethal weapon against them in the game. He wanted Dinah to create a compound that would protect them and prevent them from being affected.

"Piece of cake! I'll just pull the formula out of my ear," she said to the computer monitor which was streaming out test results that amplified the magnitude of her failure.

She raised her arms in the air in frustration then let them fall at her sides. Turning around, she walked straight into a trolley at the corner of the room, sending lab tubes and equipment shattering all over the floor.

"Ow!"

She had bumped her hip on the side of the trolley. She wasn't clumsy, but her frustration with the task at hand had cause her to be careless.

"You're such a klutz, Dinah." Her business partner grinned from the doorway.

"I'm not in a good mood, Cooper!"

He sauntered in without an invitation and sat on her lab stool. She was only five foot two, so she had adjusted the height of the stool to suit her needs. Cooper readjusted it so that his lanky body could settle comfortably. "You won't be in a good mood being around Arik."

"Well, I'll need to use that chair soon because someone has to develop a chemical compound to protect us in the upcoming multiversal hologame."

"I've been working out all night. My muscles are screaming. Can I sit for a bit?"

Dinah wagged a threatening finger at him. "I made those fake ab muscles for you. Remember that I can take them back."

He gestured up and down his torso. "They're already gone . . . when Ciaran shot at me in the market, remember? But I'm happy with the way I look now. I work out just to improve my agility."

"Jenny and her martial arts have had some good influence on you then?"

"No one can influence me. I'm always comfortable in my own skin."

Dinah rolled her eyes. "Says one who begged for fake abdomen muscles a short while ago!"

"Come on, can we not talk about that?"

"Yes, sure, if you stop calling me a klutz."

"It's a deal. Listen, I'm here to ask you for a favor."

"Naturally." Dinah rolled her eyes again. "I won't make you a love potion."

"No, that's not what I need. But if I don't get this problem figured out, no love potion will help."

Dinah frowned. "Are you okay?"

Cooper shook his head. "I've been thinking about the sound I heard when I called you from Iilos and didn't get a response."

"You said it sounded like a space creature. And it made perfect sense because we'd just had a fight before that, and they took my communication unit."

"Yes, but hear me out. I don't think it's just any sound. It was a static noise, like someone was tuning for frequency from the multiverse."

"Yes, we knew that, Cooper. Arete and his people were searching for some kind of frequency, and they had been manipulating Arik's brain waves. That was why he heard crazy music and all that."

"Yes, but I thought about it again, and it's not that simple. Or maybe it is in Arik's case. But in my case, when I played that sound again and again in my head, it started to make some sense. If I rearrange some of the tune, it's like a song. And in my last attempt, I think I got it right."

Dinah raised an eyebrow.

He sighed. "When it formed some sort of sensible tune, it shot a shock wave through my body. The energy in me surged and then subsided." He stood up and looked at her. "Unfortunately, it stayed that way. At the subsided level."

"So you lack energy? You need a vitamin shot?"

He raked his hands through his hair. "It's not that kind of energy. It's my libido."

"Cooper! You have officially crossed the line of our business partnership! You want me to help you get your rocks off?"

"Lower your voice, Dinah. Come on!"

"Cooper, I know masculine performance is important for a man. But we're on a mission here. The multiverse is in trouble. Lives are at stake. And you're worried about your libido?"

"I'm the one who's making sacrifices for the greater good here, telling you about my manliness problem and all."

"How is that sacrificing?"

"I think the control from the badasses who are hunting for the apertures has something to do with chemicals and a mind-controlling frequency. But you know that much. I also think they tried to either control or get information about something much more primal than that. Like sexual urges. I mean, think about it. In one sequence, my libido is up. Reversing it, my libido is down. And that was controlled across the cosmos."

Dinah nodded. "They're trying to control senses." She paced the room. "This is bad. Really bad. Senses rely on the immediate environment, and that's impossible to formulate without extensive simulation. That's beyond my skill set. But Ciaran can do it."

"Wait, you're not going to tell Ciaran about my libido problem, are you?"

"How else am I going to explain about the controlling of energy via multiversal frequencies?"

"Just say energy . . . or senses."

"Yes, but sexual urges are a primal sense. Those urges control human beings in a lot of ways. What if we miss out on the bigger picture by omitting that information?"

"I don't know . . ." Cooper said in frustration.

"It looks like we're having a heated debate about lab results?" Ciaran said from the doorway.

CHAPTER 2

Arik hunched down at a desk in the private apartment block of LeBlanc Pharmaceutical headquarters. He had been here before—during the time he buddied up with Ciaran and everyone else in the LeBlanc family. His mind wandered back to the time when things fell apart—he knew Ciaran had deliberately put him in this corner to prevent him from encountering staff.

He was supposed to trace back to the time he'd met the Xiilok people and figure out how Arete had played with the multiversal frequency of his brain waves. Ciaran bet Arete hit randomly at anyone who was prone to the signals.

But what would Arete's endgame be?

Arik wanted to pace the room but thought better of it, so he stayed focused on the task at hand. He was taking notes of all possible events and incidents around the time he met the yellow shield tribe in Xiilok.

Arik wasn't into computer games, let alone the multiversal hologame. He barely comprehended the concept. The multiverse was Ciaran's turf. Arik thought he could contribute in a small way by recalling and recording exactly what had happened the day he first saw the aperture. But bad memories plagued his mind and kept breaking his concentration. He closed his eyes to rest and leaned back in the chair. The clock on the wall teased.

Tick tock.

Tick tock.

It was as if the clock was counting down the time left until the multiversal hologame challenge.

He thought he had settled in as a professor at Oxford University, living his own quiet life. Apparently, someone or something out there in the cosmos didn't accept his life of peace.

He turned around, responding to a gentle knock at the door, and saw Dinah. The sight of her always refreshed and brightened his mood, no matter what his state of mind.

He still chuckled to himself when he thought about the first time they met when she had somersaulted into his lecture theater, struck a spectacular pose upon landing, flung one high-heeled red shoe at him, and unintentionally ejected one of the wings in her weaponry suit.

It had only been a short time since they'd met, but he found it hard to imagine life—after this multiversal attack event was over and he had to go to Xiilok—without Dinah in it. He'd gotten used to seeing the fragile, porcelain skin on that foxy oval face, and her pouting lips, especially when she tried to tease him or when she disagreed with him. He loved the long, black hair that wrapped around her shoulders. He was sure she intentionally brushed his skin with it whenever she walked past him, jolting his system with inexplicable sensation.

"Dinah." He smiled.

She entered the room graciously. Arik reached over and pulled a trolley of books he had just ordered from the university aside because he had some odd feeling that Dinah would bump into that hard object on her way in.

"If Ciaran has sent you, no, I haven't anything for him."

She smiled. "Yes, Ciaran sends me. But no, he didn't expect you to have anything done yet. We have a change of plans."

"Why can't he talk to me himself?"

"He was about to, but I asked if I could talk to you first."

Arik raised an eyebrow, waiting. As Dinah moved closer to him, he felt a wave rush through his body. There was nothing wrong with being attracted to a beautiful woman, but the timing was poor. Arik shook his head to clear the thoughts out of his mind.

"Why not?" Dinah asked.

"I'm sorry, what did you just say?"

"I said we should have a clear plan before you enter Mon Ciel because the history you have with Ciaran might mess with your head."

"It is now!" he muttered.

"What?"

"Never mind. So I guess Ciaran wants me to enter Mon Ciel to retrieve some information from Juliette?"

Dinah nodded.

"Why can't he do it himself? Do you know how sacred that palace is to his family?"

"He told me they have very strict security, and that he'll have to ask someone to take you in. You might know that the place is protected by a multiversal frequency shield designed to prevent any creatures from the multiverse entering."

"I know now." He sighed. "Ciaran and Madeline are Eudaizian now. That means they can't get into their own home. What a twisted fate!" Arik leaned back in his chair.

"Well, you might not be able to enter after you officially become a Xiilok tribe leader. But you're still human now, so we have a small window. But that's not why I'm here."

Arik approached. Dinah was small, and the top of her head barely reached his chest, so he lifted her up and sat her on the desk. He bent down, bracing his hands on the edge of the desk, and looked into her beautiful dark eyes. She blinked at him, and a tiny lash dropped onto her cheek. Her lips pouted slightly and parted as if inviting him to do the unthinkable.

"So why are you here? Hit me with the naked truth."

He felt as if he was outside his body, seeing himself approaching a woman without permission—the type of behavior he would only dare if he wanted a slap across the face. Or the type of thing he would have done when he was much younger.

"Arik!" she whispered with her mouth next to his ear.

"Yes," he said and turned. His lips almost touched the nape of her neck. He could feel the lust pulsing inside his body as he brushed his lips against her smooth skin.

"Arik!" she called out softly.

"Yes, Dinah!" He was going to kiss that skin.

"You're too close."

His surge of energy was brought to an abrupt halt. He jerked back, panting. "I'm sorry. I don't know why I did that." He felt out of breath and slightly dizzy.

Dinah held his shoulders. "Take it easy, Arik. That's why I'm here. And that's what I need to talk to you about."

He nodded and sat down.

Dinah continued. "In a nutshell, Ciaran believes that Juliette was working on an exotic compound before she died. And that compound might be the essential base for what I am trying without success to develop now. We don't have much time left before the challenge. So the quickest way to prepare is to get Juliette's formula, and I can work from there."

"What's the big deal here, Dinah? I can go in and grab the potion you need from Mon Ciel."

"There are two things you need to be aware of. First, Juliette didn't have the compound completed. Otherwise, Ciaran would have known. She did have the ingredients, though, and only you might be able to tell what they are."

"Me? I don't know anything about chemical compounds."

"But you do know Juliette."

Arik snorted. "Not well enough apparently."

"You were connected. Both you and Ciaran once loved that woman. And because of that connection, you will be able to tell."

"Because?"

"Because Juliette practiced alchemy."

"What?"

"Yes. Compounds or potions created from that practice have spiritual meanings that only connected people can read. And to connect back to the path of mind, you have to open up your feelings for Juliette. It' will be like opening up an old wound, and it will hurt."

Arik looked away, out the window for a moment. Then he turned back to Dinah. "All right. I can handle that. What's the second issue?"

Dinah smiled. "That's what Ciaran said. You can handle the first issue easily. The second one deals with your own emotional energy."

"Emotions again? Are you guys psychoanalyzing me like I'm a woman?"

"That's sexist, Arik."

"I'm sorry. Go on."

"You know you're prone to the multiversal frequency for some unknown reason. When you are opening up to connect with Juliette's past practice, you will be most vulnerable. Cooper had played with the frequency just a bit, and it affected his . . . let's call it his masculine performance."

Arik raised an eyebrow.

Dinah continued. "He's fine now. But he can detach the frequency from his mind, control it, and analyze it because we are not human. You are human, and you can't do what Cooper did. So if the frequency influences you, or if Arete is playing any tricks when you're in Mon Ciel—"

"I'm going cuckoo."

"Yes. And I am one hundred percent sure insanity is the result of being attacked by the multiversal frequency when opening your human emotion channels to the unknown. I don't know much about human emotions, but I'm an expert in multiversal mixed chemistry and brain waves. I know what it can do to you."

Arik paced back and forth then returned to Dinah. "So does Ciaran want me to go in or not? Why did he send you?"

"He is very sure you will accept the task if he asks you."

"Cocky bastard."

"He sent me to tell you that you have every opportunity to say no. This is not your war. And he will totally understand if you decline."

Arik approached Dinah and tilted her chin up to look into her eyes. "What do you think, Dinah?"

"I don't have an opinion on this because my mind doesn't work the same way. I know life and death, but I can't judge what it's like to lose your mind. With my makeup, it will never happen to me. But judging by how concerned Ciaran was about this, I'm saying you should decline. Also, I think you and Ciaran should decline the game, too. The most the both of you will lose is your bet."

"The bet is the Earth's population, Dinah."

"Yes, it's a lot of creatures to lose. A big bet. But you'll be the tribe leader in Xiilok. And Ciaran is king of Eudaiz, the most prosperous universe in the multiverse. Your lives are precious. Earth is only a small planet."

"You don't get it, Dinah."

"No, I'm sorry, but I don't. If the multiverse is at war, there will be losses and sacrifices. I don't understand how, when you and Ciaran got tangled up with the human issue, your great minds stopped working objectively."

"Because we're human. Regardless of whomever or whatever we might become, we were born and raised as human. Thus human interests will always be our priority."

Dinah nodded. "So what are you saying?"

He looked into her eyes and said, "I'm in."

CHAPTER 3

Madeline stepped out of the car and looked at the magnificent Mon Ciel, a palace resting imposingly on a hilltop in the exclusive area of Henley-on-Thames. The place had belonged to the LeBlanc family for a long time and bore many marks of their legacy. For her, this was the home that held many memories of Ciaran and her, of their relationship and how they had become soul mates.

The chilly breezes crept inside her jacket and made her shudder. Feeling a warm coat wrapped around her shoulders, she turned around and smiled at the sinfully handsome face of her husband—a face God had created when he was in the mood to forgive all mortal sins.

His striking gray eyes smiled back at her. "You're cold, first councillor."

Every time he called her first councillor, she wanted to swoon. But it didn't happen this time. A perk of being a mind reader was that she could occasionally peek into his mind, and those occasions tended to coincide with negative events—such as now.

A looming, dark cloud hovered over his mind. Deep concern about Arik's trip inside Mon Ciel was eating him up. Ciaran wasn't psychic, but he had excellent instincts. Whenever he sensed trouble that he could not fix, she saw those dark clouds in his mind. She made a mental note to do something about this when they returned to Eudaiz. She needed to train herself to see his mind when he was happy.

Behind them, other cars arrived and parked about one hundred yards away from Mon Ciel's fence. Arik, Dinah, Cooper, Jenny, and Lindsay exited these cars. This was a major event for people from the multiverse. However, because people on Earth were oblivious to it, Ciaran wanted to keep it low key.

Madeline entwined her fingers with Ciaran's and felt a slight squeeze from his hand. They both looked toward Mon Ciel. Not long ago, they'd fought supernatural creatures together, and Mon Ciel had been a safe haven for them. Now, looking at the palace from the outside, they saw a shield hovering over it like a dome.

The very shield that had protected them now prevented them from entering their own home.

Ciaran turned around. He rubbed his thumb over the dimple on her left cheek and smiled at her. "We have a new home now."

She nodded. "Yes, I love our new home. So whatever you do, make sure we return there. Our children are waiting."

"I'm sure we will." He kissed her lightly and turned toward the approaching group of people, leaving her standing there with a gigantic knot in her stomach.

Ciaran approached Lindsay.

Madeline recalled vividly the night she was attacked just outside London when Ciaran came to the rescue, a trip that had cost him his head of security and best friend's life. Lindsay was Ciaran's right-hand man at LeBlanc Pharmaceuticals. After that incident, he had tightened security and had always been there for Ciaran without fail. For

Ciaran, Lindsay was more than just a subordinate. Lindsay was a friend—a part of his inner circle.

"I appreciate you helping me with this, Lindsay."

"Do you have to say that, Ciaran?"

"I understand it's difficult for you to escort Arik inside Mon Ciel given what happened in the past. But I don't trust anyone else to do this job."

"Understood."

Ciaran patted Lindsay's shoulder. "I owe you one."

"Don't mention it." Lindsay pulled out his cell phone and gave it to Ciaran. "Guard it with your life! My wife gave it to me." Lindsay grinned and returned to his car.

Ciaran walked toward Arik. "Once you're inside, I'll give you instructions on what to look for."

"How? Are you going to give me one of those fancy wrist units of yours?"

"No, it would be wiped clean when it goes past the protective shield. Lindsay has to leave his cell phone with me. You see?"

"Bloody hell, how much security do you need for a palace?" Arik exclaimed. Then he saw the look on Ciaran's face. "All right, I'll get in and out in one piece."

Ciaran nodded. "Thanks. I appreciate it. Once you're inside, Lindsay will get you a primitive piece of technology called a cell phone. Then I can call you from his phone and give you instructions."

"All right."

"Just to be sure, when you look at Mon Ciel now, you don't see a glowing, dome-shaped shield, do you?"

"Nope. It looks like just another castle in the English countryside. I'm not suicidal. If I saw the shield, I wouldn't put my neck through it. Trust me. Just out of curiosity, what would it do to you and other space creatures?"

"Electrocution. Burned toast. Barbecue. However you want to describe it."

"I get the picture."

Ciaran snapped a wristband onto Arik's wrist.

"Ouch!"

"If his band flashes, back the car right out. Don't go through the shield," Ciaran told Lindsay, who had settled into the driver's seat and started the car.

"Copy that."

The car moved slowly toward the gate, which automatically opened and cleared them in. Before the gate closed, Arik turned around and gave them a thumbs-up.

"Phew!" Cooper exhaled loudly.

Jenny chuckled. "I didn't know you cared about my brother that much."

"Oh, I don't. I'm just worried about the car."

Madeline wrapped her arms around Ciaran from behind. She didn't sense him feeling any easier. "What's wrong, Ciaran?"

"I don't know. I haven't figured it out yet."

From the corner of her eye, she saw Dinah looking anxiously at her wrist unit. She looked as agitated as Ciaran.

Ciaran's unit beeped, and he engaged immediately. "Talk to me, Jake."

Jake was head of intelligence in Eudaiz. He was very young to hold such an important position. But Ciaran trusted Jake's capability and integrity. Jake had proven Ciaran correct on several occasions.

"I'm calling you because the wristband you've used has been compromised. It's just been activated now, and it flashed on my screen."

Dinah rushed over. "What does that mean, Ciaran?"

"Which part was compromised, Jake?" Ciaran asked.

"The broadcasting function."

"It's going to broadcast manipulative frequencies!" Dinah teared up. "Can you call Arik now, Ciaran?"

Ciaran shook his head. "It's too late. I have to go in."

"Ciaran!" Madeline exclaimed although she knew Ciaran would ignore her.

He looked at Jake's image on the screen. "Send me TX25."

Jake's eyebrows shot up. "But it's a prototype."

"It's been tested. Park the capsule in the cross-dimension." Ciaran's face hardened, and his eyes were as cold as steel. Madeline knew there was nothing she could say that would stop him from going inside. As she had done countless times before, she closed her eyes, concentrated, and forced her precognition and mind tracking abilities to work hard, hoping to find a solution.

CHAPTER 4

Arik's mouth hung agape for a moment when he saw the magnificence of Mon Ciel from the inside. In front of him were endless marble hallways, columns, decorative statues, and splendid works of art. But unlike other castles and palaces he had seen in England, behind the grandeur of Mon Ciel was a sense of home.

Now he understood why Juliette had no hesitation in calling this place home after she married Ciaran. He sighed. Dinah was right, opening old wounds was never easy. He should get past that state now. But for the purpose of the task at hand, he let the feelings linger.

He was supposed to channel Juliette's emotional energy. Normally, he would laugh at the ludicrous suggestion. But based on what had happened in the last few weeks, it might be the most sensible solution.

Something in his mind just clicked. It felt as if a pathway had been cleared. His mind's eyes saw a light at the end of the hallway. Whatever it was that Dinah had suggested seemed to work. Arik concentrated.

The light flickered a couple of times and then vanished. He shook his head and tried to relax, thinking about the palace and Juliette. The light appeared again.

"Arik!" Lindsay called out.

"Yes."

"We need to go and get the phone so Ciaran can give you instructions."

"Okay, you go. I'll stay right here," Arik said and focused on the light. He didn't want the vision to go away, and he was sure Lindsay didn't see it.

"I can't let you stay here by yourself. I promised Ciaran I'd get you out in one piece."

"No one's here. You think these marble statues are going to jump out and bite me? If you need to get the phone, go get it."

"Why can't you go with me? The equipment room is in the upper wing." Lindsay pointed toward the left.

Arik glanced to the right and saw the hovering light. "Where is Juliette's lab?"

"At the lower end." Lindsay pointed toward the light he couldn't see. "I can get you there after we get the phone. You need to talk to Ciaran because I don't have the code to get in."

"Right," Arik muttered and turned to follow Lindsay. But as soon as he turned, the light disappeared. "Oh no! Okay, how about I go to the lab now, and you go and get the phone."

"What's wrong with you? I told you I can't let you go to that wing by yourself."

"All right, why don't we go to the lab, and I'll see if I can figure out a way in and take the information myself. If I can't, then we'll come back for the phone."

"Why?"

"Can't tell you why. But I'm going to the lab now." Arik turned toward the right and walked along the corridor.

Lindsay muttered in protest but then followed.

Beside an imposing steel door was a keypad that glared at Arik in challenge. The light had taken him here, but it hadn't given him the code. Maybe he needed to go with Lindsay to the equipment room for the phone after all. A tingling sensation shot through this body, coming from the wristband Ciaran had given him. This must be one of Ciaran's tricks, giving him the code without telling him.

Arik stared at the keypad. A short moment later, the code illuminated on the keyboard. Arik followed the prompts. When he pressed the last digit, he heard a click, and the door slid open.

"Well, at least I didn't have to say open sesame," Arik muttered and entered the lab. Hundreds of colorful jars, tubes, and God knows what kind of lab equipment filled the room. Now he was seriously considering getting Ciaran's instructions. He squared his shoulders and concentrated.

He let his mind wander back to the time he and Juliette were lovers. It was a good time. He could see her beautiful face and flaming red hair. They were so young. She smiled at him. He remembered the vibrant energy that emanated from her body. She loved life, art, and nature.

He could see her walking through the field of wildflowers when they visited her hometown in

Ireland. She inhaled the fragrance of the grass and flowers. She looked at them as if she knew them. She could talk to the wildflowers. She whispered something he couldn't hear.

"What's that, Juliette?" he asked.

She smiled and picked a bunch of wildflowers. "These are my favorite."

"Okay, let me get some more for you." He reached out to the flowers, and his hand hit a cold jar. He jerked his hand back, and the jar fell from his hand. Then his world went black. Soon after, he opened his eyes and found himself on the lab floor.

Lindsay held a jar of potion in his hand, looking at him with concern. "Are you okay? You just passed out and almost dropped this jar on the floor. I don't know anything about these potions. But I know we don't want to be near a broken jar."

Arik sat up. "Let me try again."

"Try what? Let's go get the phone."

"No, I have a sensation. Like a feeling of what might be the right potion. If we leave now, I'm not sure I can get that sensation back."

Lindsay nodded. "All right, I'll stay right here to make sure you don't break anything." Lindsay went and stood next to the door as if ready to jump out of the way if Arik broke anything in the lab.

Arik nodded and concentrated again. Images of Juliette flooded back to his mind—so fresh and so real. It felt like only yesterday that they were together.

He could feel his own movements in the lab. In a while, the memories seemed to subside. He didn't feel the need to remember or do anything more. His mind was flung back to reality.

He looked down at the lab table. Several jars of potions and powders were opened. There were signs of an experiment completed. He saw traces of colored powder on his hands. And he was holding a jar of liquid potion.

He knew this was the compound they needed. He stared at the light blue and purple liquid in the jar.

Then Arik felt a gun muzzle pressing against his temple.

"Put the jar down," Lindsay said.

CHAPTER 5

Madeline paced back and forth and around. Her psychic abilities had once again decided to abandon her when she needed them most. Jake had delivered TX25, the prototype capsule. Although she couldn't see the vehicle because he had parked it in the cross-dimensional section, she was sure it would be like the other capsules in Eudaiz—egg-shaped, the size of a minibus, and made of an unusually resilient material she didn't know the name of.

Ciaran had designed this model for combat, though, so she figured it would be smaller in size to maximize its flexibility. It would most likely be able to tolerate weaponry attacks more than an ordinary capsule. But Mon Ciel's shield wouldn't be easily breached. Ciaran's family had designed and built it, and for decades, it had deterred numerous space creatures.

Ciaran crossed in and out of this dimension, adjusting his wrist unit and utilizing a portable keyboard. She knew he was navigating the capsule. She wished she could cross dimensions to see what he was doing on the other side. But at the moment, all she could do to help was to will her psychic ability and precognition to work so she could partially predict what might happen.

Ciaran stepped back into the current dimension, his eyes focused on the portable control panel to make further adjustments. Dinah lurked close by, asking to join him. But when it came to critical moments like this, Ciaran trusted only himself.

He looked up from the control panel as if he had finished his preparation. His eyes scanned quickly over the group standing nearby. Madeline knew he would be looking for her, so she made sure she was right there for him.

She approached quickly, kissed him lightly, and smiled. "I love you."

He didn't smile back. As usual, his striking gray eyes grew intense. He wiped away a tear on her face she didn't know had fallen. "I love you, too. And I'm sorry for doing this."

"You have to do what you have to do. Otherwise, you wouldn't be the man I love."

"I haven't tested this. But in theory, a cross-dimensional detour would get me past the shield. Do you trust me?"

She shook her head and looked straight up into his eyes. "Not this time. But I trust my instincts. My precognition always flares up if you're in trouble. It's been quiet, so I believe you'll be fine." She smiled at him.

He kissed her then said, "I'll be back shortly. Wait for me here, first councillor." He strode toward the left, and then, in a flash, he vanished into the cross-dimension.

Madeline turned around, rubbing her stomach absently.

Dinah approached. "You couldn't get your psychic abilities to work, could you?"

Madeline wiped a tear away. "No."

Jenny said, "Thank you for letting Ciaran go inside for my brother."

Madeline shook her head. "Don't thank me too soon."

She looked toward the horizon. Something flashed in her mind.

"To the creek!" she shouted, pointing toward the creek at the base of the hill. She had been to that creek several times. She had just seen a flash of light in her precognition. She couldn't quite make sense of it yet, so she just followed her sixth sense—another perk of being a psychic—and figured the shiny flash was the water.

***

In the lab, Arik looked sideways, straight into the gun's muzzle. "A toy gun?" he scoffed.

Lindsay used the gun barrel to swing at Arik's temple, sending him staggering back and almost causing him to pass out.

"It's plastic, designed for me to pass the shield. But I can guarantee you it's not a toy. I suggest you not try my temper again." Lindsay grinned crookedly and brandished the gun. "Now put the jar down."

"No."

Lindsay pointed the gun at Arik's leg, but before he could shoot, Arik wagged a finger with his free hand.

"You're smart enough to know who is holding a more dangerous weapon here. If I drop this jar, we'll both die. So I suggest you not try *my* temper. I'm known to have one, if your memory is good."

Arik raised an eyebrow in challenge. When Lindsay didn't make a move, Arik continued. "Ciaran trusts you. Why are you doing this?"

"I have never betrayed Ciaran. But you and I don't stand on the same ground. He can only choose one of us. Apparently, he chose you. And that's a huge mistake."

"So all this is just to prove a point?"

Lindsay fired at a wall. The silenced gun dug a large hole in the solid brick. "My sister isn't a point to prove."

"It was an accident."

"The hell it was. If you hadn't seduced Liz with that pretty face of yours just to get back at Ciaran for taking Juliette, my sister would still be alive. She was sixteen. Do you have any fucking compassion?" Lindsay fired at the wall again.

"As you said, Liz was sixteen. I couldn't stop her from having feelings for me. She OD'd, and that had nothing to do with whatever happened between Ciaran and me . . ."

Lindsay fired at Arik's left shoulder. Arik staggered back, his arm swung up, and the jar slipped out of his hand. Lindsay darted over and grabbed the jar midair.

Lindsay looked at the jar and smirked. "Who's the loser now?" he asked. He aimed the gun at Arik's head. "I'd let you live if you showed any sign of remorse about my sister's death. But I know you have no regrets about letting my sister die."

Sweat trickled down Arik's forehead, and blood seeped out between the fingers of the hand with which he clutched his wound.

"You're a fucking scumbag. Liz was innocent, and her death was a tragedy. But now you use your sister's death for money?"

"Shut the fuck up!" Lindsay thrust the gun muzzle forward but didn't pull the trigger.

"Your sister is just an excuse. If you wanted to put a bullet in my head, you would have done it by now. What else did they pay you for, apart from getting that jar? Is there something in me? In my head?"

"Scan your wristband against all the other jars. Do it now."

Arik grabbed at his band, about to yank it off.

"It's the only thing keeping you alive. Ciaran coded it for you. And you can only operate it when you're alive. If you take it off, I'll shoot you with pleasure. Now scan the rest of the lab."

Arik stood still. "I don't understand the LeBlanc's secrets. But I know if you sell them, many people will die. They are betting on Earth's population right now . . ."

"It's not my problem. All I want now is to blow your head off. So scan the fuck out of the lab!"

They heard a low growl, and a shadow darted in, hitting Lindsay hard from behind. Lindsay fell to the floor, almost losing consciousness. Ciaran stood tall, holding the jar in his hand.

Arik had never seen so much rage in Ciaran, and he was sure Ciaran's supernatural power was activated at the moment.

"Take it off!" Ciaran pointed at Arik's wristband. Arik yanked off the band and stomped his foot on it without mercy.

On the floor, Lindsay looked up. "I'm sorry, Ciaran. I never meant to betray you."

"Apology not accepted," Ciaran said and turned toward Arik.

"Look out!" Arik yelled as he saw Lindsay scramble to his feet and pull something from his sock.

Ciaran whirled around and had Lindsay at gunpoint.

Lindsay held a small round device the size of a coin in his open palm.

"An ordinary gun cannot get past Mon Ciel security. You know that better than anyone else, Ciaran. But this explosive device isn't any ordinary weapon. I never planned to betray you until you brought that prick who killed my sister back into your life. Now put the gun down and give me back the jar, Ciaran," Lindsay said to Ciaran while watching Arik's every movement.

"You really disappoint me, Lindsay." Ciaran lowered the gun and dropped it to the floor. His left hand still held the jar.

"I'm sorry, Ciaran," Lindsay said.

"You're sorry to take a prize on my head?"

Lindsay chuckled bitterly. "I didn't know you'd come in here for him. Again, you're choosing him over my lifetime of devotion to the LeBlancs. What has he ever done for your friendship, if there ever was a friendship?"

"I've never sold him short, at any price. I top you on that," Arik said.

"I'm not talking to you!" Lindsay shouted at Arik. Seeing he was distracted, Ciaran seized the opportunity to plant a kick on his abdomen, sending him to the floor. The round device slid out of his hand, rolling on the floor and flashing a red light.

Arik was no expert in weapons, but judging by the look on Lindsay's face, he knew there was no way anyone in this room was going to get out in one piece. He darted toward the device. He might be able to lessen the damage with his body. He couldn't think of any other solution.

But Ciaran was right behind him. He could feel Ciaran's strong hold on his jacket, pulling him back.

"Don't!" Ciaran shouted.

On the floor, Lindsay rolled over and lay on top of the device. He looked up at Ciaran. "They want the primer, Ciaran. Please protect my family."

That was all Arik saw and felt. There was a whirl of white particles in front of him, and then the pressure from the blast.

CHAPTER 6

Flying was officially her most favorite skill now, Dinah thought while running as fast as she could, following Madeline down the hill toward the creek. Madeline had switched on her supernatural power—one she referred to as the silver blood or the special eudqi. Although Ciaran had not had a chance to master a way to utilize the silver blood, at the moment, it allowed Madeline to accentuate her natural talent. Madeline was running like the wind.

Dinah didn't exactly fly naturally like a bird. She had to use the wings in her weaponry suit. But she considered the ability to leap in the air and surf in the wind at incredible speeds with the artificial wings an important skill. That was good enough, she thought.

Damn, that was good! Dinah thought as she looked to the sky in the direction Madeline was pointing. She would kill for Madeline's psychic ability.

From the empty sky, an egg-shaped vehicle appeared. It was as if it had just torn through some kind of dimensional curtain and penetrated this dimension. It was in flame. Two objects were ejected from it, and then the capsule exploded into nothingness.

"Hello and goodbye TX25," Dinah muttered. She knew by now the two flying objects were Ciaran and Arik being ejected out of the burning capsule.

One of their parachutes had been released. The other person had no parachute and free-fell.

"Oh no!" she cried out.

Madeline saw it, too. They had closed the distance a little more, and they could tell who was who was who.

"That's Arik!" Madeline shouted, pointing at the falling person.

Dinah veered in Arik's direction.

Arik was free-falling fast.

The wind was strong. It pushed Ciaran's parachute in another direction. In front of their astonished eyes, Ciaran ripped off his parachute and free-fell toward Arik.

"Arik isn't conscious!" Madeline shouted.

"Goddammit," Dinah cursed and spread her wings.

Ciaran closed the distance with Arik, and once he grabbed Arik's hand, he ejected his second emergency parachute. It took off with the wind, but they still descended rapidly toward the fast-running creek down the hill.

Dinah changed her flight path.

On the ground, Madeline had changed direction so that when Ciaran and Arik landed on the bank of the creek, she would be right there.

The creek dropped down about fifty feet, and a hanging bridge hung precariously from one side to the other. The wind carried Ciaran's parachute, crashing it into the bridge and tangling it in the bridge's steel wires. Before Ciaran could do anything, Madeline was on the bridge, charging toward them.

The parachute was tearing with the weight of the two men dangling in the strong wind. Arik was dead weight as he was still unconscious. Ciaran couldn't climb up with one hand on the tearing parachute and the other hand holding Arik.

Madeline dove over and grabbed Ciaran's hand before it slid off the parachute. The momentum pushed her over the edge of the bridge. She dangled by one hand with the weight of two men below her.

"Let go of my hand, Madeline!" Ciaran shouted.

"It's too high to drop to the water," Madeline said.

"I can take care of both of us, but not if you fall, too. Let go."

"No. Dinah will come soon."

"We're too heavy for her."

"I can't let go of you two. It's too high to fall from here. We need another lifter. Dinah can help."

Before Madeline could say anything further, the weight caused her to lose her grip on the bridge. The three of them fell but still hung together like a human string, flying in the wind.

Dinah flew over and grabbed Madeline's hand just before gravity dragged them all down. She flapped her wings rapidly, but the wings designed to carry her tiny body couldn't lift the weight of three additional people in addition to the force of the strong wind. They descended rapidly downward to the cold water, heading toward a small waterfall a hundred yards in front of them.

"Just slow our falling speed to lessen the impact when we hit. We should be okay to swim when we get to the water," Ciaran shouted up.

"That's the plan," Dinah responded, cursing the rainwater smashing into her face. She had to use both hands to get a good grip on Madeline's hand, so she didn't have a spare hand to wipe the moisture from her eyes. She couldn't see where they were flying. But she knew it was downward.

"Arik is heating up!" Ciaran called from below her.

"How many times already? You think he'll travel?" Madeline asked.

"I don't know how many times. But it doesn't matter—I think he'll travel very soon," Ciaran said.

Dinah knew Ciaran was right. Whenever Arik's body heated up, he time traveled, carrying whoever was in contact with him through the time travel as well. It had happened before with Madeline. Time traveling would be fun if Arik were in control of it. It was bad enough that he couldn't control it when he was conscious. Now, being unconscious, Dinah had no idea where this would take them.

Ciaran called again, "I can't let go of Arik. If he drops to the water now, he'll drown. Let go of my hand, Madeline."

"If he travels, I'll have to go with you. I can mind navigate. You can't," Madeline said.

Dinah flapped her wings harder, but it didn't help the situation. If they landed faster, as soon as they were on safe ground, Ciaran could let go of Arik's hand. Dinah folded her wings and stopped flying.

They fell faster.

But it was too late.

She saw a flash of white light coming from beneath them. And then everything turned white.

CHAPTER 7

Helpless. Cooper cursed himself, letting out a stream of profanity he didn't know he was capable of while running toward the creek. He couldn't compare himself to Ciaran or Madeline. They had supernatural power—he didn't. Dinah had no magical power, but she could fly with her artificial wings. She was very helpful and could do amazing things he couldn't.

"Damn it."

He cursed again at the fact that he was forced to run on the ground like an ordinary human being. Jenny almost beat him in the race to the creek. He could see Ciaran in the distance, and Arik and

Dinah flew through the air in scattered flying paths that made no sense to him. He ran in the general direction of the creek and darted over to the edge. Jenny flopped down next to him.

About twenty feet below, Arik, Ciaran, Madeline, and Dinah vanished into thin air.

"Shit! They've time traveled," he muttered.

"What?" Jenny asked incredulously.

"Calm down. They've done it before. Arik has done it countless times and returned safely. Last time, he brought Madeline with him, and they both came back just fine. So you don't have to worry. Your brother *will* return safely."

"Cooper?"

"Yes, Jenny."

"You're the one who needs to calm down."

"Oh, right. Okay, we'll just stay here and wait."

Cooper knew if he went into his normal brooding mode right now, number one, it wouldn't help the situation, and number two, it worried him how it would affect Jenny's thoughts of him. There was no room for worries now. He had to do what he always did best to save his friends—investigate. "I have to Toogle," he said.

"You have to what?"

"I have to search a multiversal open data portal. I have a theory about what's happening."

"So it's like Googling. I mean . . . searching for an Internet data portal on Earth."

Cooper shrugged and switched on his wrist unit.

"What's your theory? Is there anything I can do to help?" Jenny asked.

"Well, Arete challenged Ciaran, Eudaiz, and Arik to the hologame, betting on the Earth's population to make them sweat. I originally thought he was taking advantage of Ciaran's and Arik's connection to humans. But now I think Arete himself has connections to both humans and the multiverse. Also, he was looking for something very specific inside Mon Ciel. Something that might connect to the past. That's why he manipulated Arik's brainwaves and made him time travel."

"My brother must have found whatever Arete was looking for inside Mon Ciel, and that thing triggered his travel."

Cooper nodded. "Yes, it's a possibility. But their manipulation of Arik's wristband was done in Eudaiz, right in Ciaran's backyard. Infiltrating the Eudaizian system is almost impossible, so I'm thinking this is quite an elaborate scheme, much larger than the hologame challenge. And Arete might not be the key player."

"So the multiversal hologame might be just a decoy?"

"Precisely." Cooper sighed. "I think Arete's endgame crosses multiple worlds."

Jenny frowned. "I thought the multiverse crossed multiple worlds already . . . "

"Not necessarily. I'm not an expert on metaphysical matters. We're better off discussing this with Ciaran . . . if we can find him."

"It looks like we're not the only ones wanting to find him." Jenny tilted her chin toward a stretch of land on the middle of the hillside halfway down to the creek.

Cooper squinted. "Indeed," he said.

A space creature in human shape was searching the area where their friends had just vanished into another time dimension. As they spoke, the creature's head jerked up, and its striking yellow eyes stared straight at them.

Cooper immediately pulled Jenny back from the edge of the cliff, just before the creature leaped into the air and landed right in front of them. It stood tall, upright. Its shape flickered several times then settled as an eight-foot-tall man with an ancient face, long gray hair, and dark, evil eyes.

Sensing Jenny wanted to step forward, Cooper shoved her back behind him. He would face her wrath later, but this creature wasn't ordinary. There was no way he'd let her fight it, even with her earthly martial arts skills.

"So you can fly without wings. Any other tricks?" he asked.

"Where did they go?" the man croaked out in a strange voice.

"Why do you look like you're from *Lord of the Rings* but speak like you're from *Planet of the Apes*?" Jenny asked.

"What does that even mean?" Cooper asked.

The man growled. "I am not an ape."

Jenny spoke between clenched teeth to Cooper, "I'm just buying time. How fast can you run?"

"I'm not going to run!"

"Where did they go, Cooper Donovan?"

Cooper turned and looked at the creature. *It knew his name.* He'd better be careful. The creature in an old man's form might be able to read minds. He refrained from any further thoughts.

"Well, I know where they've gone. But if I tell you, I'm sure you'll kill us, Arete."

The old man smirked, and his face seemed to grow even more ancient. Cooper could tell Arete was impressed.

Cooper continued, "You've done your homework, so there's no point in me beating around the bush. I don't care at all what you want with the hologame. I'm on a job and got tangled up in this mess. If you compensate me for my loss of income and agree to let my business partner return to Iilos safely, I'll tell you where they've gone."

"Agreed," Arete said.

"Well, I can't take you on your word. I need it in writing. And I need the money wired immediately. Now. I take multiversal currency."

"How much do you want?"

"A hundred thousand."

Arete smirked again. "No problem."

Cooper nodded and grinned. He pulled out an electronic notepad. "All right, sign here. My account number is there. I need proof of a successful transaction before I'll give you any information."

Arete nodded. Cooper gave him the pad. As soon as they were within arm's reach, Cooper pulled his gun and shot Arete in the face. The laser cut a hole in Arete's head, from the front to the back. Cooper fired again, and this time, the beam sliced off half his head.

Arete's body sparked with electric current. Then he crumbled to the ground, and his body disintegrated.

"You've killed—"

Before Jenny could finish her sentence, Cooper grabbed her hand and charged toward an inland field.

"What are you doing?" Jenny asked while following him.

"I don't have the money for an express or exclusive vessel. We'll have to catch the public multiversal transport. You have to come with me to Iilos. Once we're inside the border, we'll be protected. Those shots destroyed Arete's body for now, but he'll return again very soon."

"You're saying he's invincible?"

"Not invincible . . . I just don't know how to kill him."

"How do we get to the transport?"

Cooper stopped running. He turned around and held Jenny's hands. "Do you trust me?"

She looked into his eyes. "Yes."

"Okay, I'll take you the way I came. It won't be glamorous. But it's relatively safe. Ready?"

She nodded.

"Close your eyes."

She followed his instructions.

He kissed her cheek quickly then teleported to the transitional zone of the multiverse, grinning foolishly on the way.

CHAPTER 8

Madeline opened her eyes, immediately registering the unfamiliar surroundings and the time-traveling experience. Unlike the previous trip with Arik where they had been transported to the past in an instant without losing consciousness, this time was different. It seemed as if they had traveled through a passage of emptiness. There had been no sound, no sense of anything—and certainly there were no memories.

She sat right up and saw a small bushland on the right and a hillside sloping slightly toward the left. She couldn't tell where they were, but she was sure they were no longer in England.

Then she felt the pain. It wasn't from the travel. It was from loss—the emptiness of losing something very important in her life. She couldn't figure out what the exact feeling was, but she knew she had experienced it before—and had no desire to feel it again. There were both perks and curses when you were a psychic. And her current experience was the latter.

Arik and Dinah sprung to their feet, panting.

"We just time traveled as a group. It's okay. Don't freak out," Arik said.

"I'm not. We were flying in the air just a moment ago, and I'm just a bit disoriented. You were unconscious. Do you know where you've transported us?" Dinah asked.

"You're bleeding, Arik," Madeline said.

Arik tugged at the collar of his shirt and looked at his shoulder. There were bloodstains on his shirt. The hole on the shirt made it look as if he'd been shot, but he saw no wound. "Well, I guess only my shirt was hurt," he said.

Madeline looked down and saw Ciaran on the ground. Her feeling of loss started to make sense. The last time she had experienced that sensation was at the finality of the Daimon Gate tests with

Ciaran—when she saw him die in front of her, and there was nothing she could do about it.

The pain of the memories was terrifying.

In front of Mon Ciel, both she and Ciaran had their eudqi on to enhance their power. That was how Ciaran had been able to shoot through the air holding Arik, and that was how she had gotten to them at the creek in time. She was sure her eudqi was off now. She flopped to the ground, yanked Ciaran's shirt open at the chest, and saw the faint mark of his eudqi point intact.

So he's fine. He isn't dead. She exhaled in relief.

"Is he injured?" Dinah asked.

"Not physically. But I don't know what's going on." Madeline shook Ciaran's shoulders. "Come on, Ciaran."

"Can you tell where we are now, Arik?" Dinah asked.

Arik was surveying the landscape. He shook his head. "Too hard to tell with the trees and grass. It all looks the same. Animals would look the same, too. If we saw a dinosaur running out from that bush, that would be different, but here, I need to see people and some buildings or some kind of civil activities to tell the era."

On the ground, Ciaran stirred.

"There you are!" Madeline helped him sit up. He looked around groggily.

Dinah crouched. "How are you feeling?" she asked. "You must have hit your head on the flight!" She smiled with concern.

Ciaran smiled back politely and rubbed his head. Madeline helped him stand up. He swayed a bit and then steadied himself. He looked at Dinah again and then Arik, and then he looked back at Madeline.

"Thanks, Lucy. This is embarrassing. How did I hit my head?" Ciaran said to Madeline with a heavy American accent.

"Excuse me?" Madeline said.

Ciaran lowered his voice, glancing at Arik and Dinah. "Are they the secret contacts you talked about, Lucy?"

Madeline was speechless.

Arik immediately figured out what was going on. He approached quickly, reaching his hand out to Ciaran for a handshake. "Arik. Nice to meet you. No, we're just friends. Not secret contacts." He offered a wide grin.

"Robert," Ciaran said and shook Arik's hand.

Dinah shoved her way in, standing in front of Madeline, and reached her hand out as well. "Dinah

Greenwoods. I'm sure we've met before. You're one of the Donovans, right?"

Ciaran, as Robert, chuckled. "Oh no, if I had met a beautiful lady like you, I would certainly remember. I'm a Lincoln."

"Oh fuck!" Arik exclaimed.

When Ciaran raised an eyebrow, Arik gave an apology. "I've left my travel documentation at the hotel. I put it in the safe then forgot about it when I checked out."

Madeline's head was spinning—as was her world. This was unprecedented—the fact that people who time traveled with Arik took on real roles in the past. *Did that mean they couldn't come back to 2017 from whatever year it was now?*

When Ciaran died at the Daimon Gate, it was the physical loss of him that pained her. She didn't know what kind of loss this was. What was she to him at this moment, as Lucy? Were they together? Judging by his manner, Lucy and Robert weren't exactly intimate.

Unsure how to handle the situation and the role she was supposed to take, she looked away, trying to avoid conversation.

Ciaran said, "All right, although I don't know where we are and why we're wearing these strange clothes, I'm going to take Lucy home first and then give you a lift to the hotel."

He turned toward Madeline, thinking she was Lucy, and gave her the crook of his elbow. "Ready to go home, Ms. Hale?"

Madeline smiled and glanced quickly at Arik and Dinah. If they were to hail a taxi, she would be in trouble. *Where does Lucy live? Who is she?*

Madeline summoned all her energy and willed a psychic channel into Arik's mind, hoping for some information. It bounced. *Damn.*

She did it again with Dinah. Dinah clicked. Madeline sent her message, channeling to Dinah's mind. *I have no idea what to do,* she said. *I can't take him to a home I don't know!*

Dinah winked. Getting the hint, Madeline peeked into Dinah's mind again and saw a word—*faint.*

Madeline slumped to the ground, pretending to pass out. She heard Dinah's voice say, "Oh dear, I told her she had to drink more water. This play consumes a lot of energy."

"She was dehydrated? Are you sure? I dislike the idea of bringing her to the hospital," Ciaran said.

"Yes, I'm sure," Dinah said. "She needs only rest."

"I'll take her home. Her father has access to the best private doctors."

"I don't think she'd like that."

"What do you mean, Dinah?"

"She told me they've just had a disagreement. She didn't say what it was about, but I'm sure she wouldn't want to be taken home like this."

"All right. I'll take her to my place."

"Is it nearby?" Arik asked.

"I have no idea where we are, but let's get to the road."

Madeline felt herself lifted, and then she was held comfortably in the familiar arms of her husband.

"I'll get my document later. Let me give you a hand with this," Arik said.

"I'll call for our family doctor when we get home."

"No need. I'm a doctor," Arik said.

"And I'm a nurse," Dinah said.

"Right then. I won't call the doctor. But what were we doing in the bush at this time of day? Which play were you talking about?"

"You don't remember anything?" Dinah asked.

"No, unfortunately. As you've said, I must have hit my head hard. I was talking to Lucy in the courtyard at my place. She said she wanted me to meet someone. Then this. I don't remember anything else."

"But you remember your name," Dinah said. "Wrong one anyway."

"Excuse me?" Ciaran asked.

Arik cut in, "We were rehearsing a play . . . it's a futuristic story. Hence the strange clothes." Arik said. "It's amateurish, of course. We're doing it for charity, to support your father's campaign. And you're not playing. You were just standing in today."

"Of course. I'm no good at acting," Ciaran muttered, his eyes darkening a shade.

"Oh, an animal-powered vehicle is coming!" Dinah shouted.

"That's what it's called in the play," Arik cut in. "She means a carriage. Dinah takes her part very seriously."

CHAPTER 9

Charmine awakened and stared straight up at the stone ceiling of a dark cell that reeked of mold, rotten corpses, and sewage. She didn't know which smell was worse, but it didn't matter. Thirst burned her throat, but she would rather go to hell than drink the water in the puddle next to her, formed by the water trickling down from above. She could feel a chilled toxic mist seeping up from the floor. Someone or something was chanting from above. The humming noise of a praying crowd crept into the cell. She must be underground.

She moved her body. The pain stabbing at her brain told her she was very much alive. She rubbed gently at her tummy.

"How are you, my sweet child?" She refused to believe their child hadn't survived.

She recalled vividly how she had plunged the knife into her evil sorceress sister for the second time. There was no dark magic that could save Luna from that injury. Charmine didn't regret many things in life . . . until now. And it wasn't killing her sister.

She should have taken her apprenticeship in the house of Gods more seriously. That would have stopped Luna from cursing their child. Or at least she would have known how to break the curse.

She sat up in her cell. Her mind was crystal clear despite her body being numb with agony. Luna had broken her right leg, twisted her flesh and bone into an unrecognizable mess. Dried blood stains clung to her white dress, rubbing at whatever was left of her skin. She used her arms to push herself to a sitting position against the wall.

Who had saved her and then locked her in here? she wondered.

Charmine knew that with a stab wound so severe, Luna was dead. But she didn't know the spiritual consequences of her actions. Then, just before her world blurred into oblivion, someone had stood behind her and ripped Luna's heart out with bare hands—or claws.

A monster? Charmine shook her head. It couldn't be. Why her? She had nothing to give anyone except for a soon-to-be-swollen tummy. She had no profession, no possessions, no magic, and no other supernatural power whatsoever.

She sighed. "What would you like to do when you grow up, child? Do you want to be an angel like your father?" She couldn't help but smile when she thought of her husband. She refused to believe he was dead. Luna had lied to her. All she had was a bloody feather. Jael would come to save her and their child. He was an angel, and his family was most important for him to protect.

But she needed to protect herself until he came for her. Angels couldn't bring you back from death. She knew that much by eavesdropping on important meetings in the house of Gods.

A door slid open at the far end of the dark dungeon, and two men in long hooded cloaks walked in.

Now she could see clearer. Along that dungeon hall were the cells of other prisoners. She wasn't sure what kind of creatures they were, but they reached out their hands—or things that looked like hands, maybe tentacles—and tried to grab the two men. The men ignored them and walked straight to her cell.

From outside the steel barred wall, they stood and looked at her. It was too dark for her to make out their faces.

"She's awake now," one croaked out.

"Where am I? What do you want from me?"

"And she speaks," the other man said.

"I'm not speaking—I'm asking questions. I ask, and you answer. That's communication based on the house of Gods' etiquette. You don't want to disrespect me and anger the Gods," she said.

Both men laughed.

"She's quite a tough bitch, isn't she?" one man said.

"It's a pity we don't care about her. So what do you think? Is she tough enough that the curse didn't work on the child?"

The other man shook his head. "Hard to tell. I'll check with Master. He always knows what to do."

"I need clean clothes, water, and a clean bed!" Charmine demanded.

The other man chuckled. "She's funny, too."

A loud bang echoed in the dungeon, and sounds of panic, chaos, and fear followed.

"Shit, what is that?" a man asked.

"Whatever it is, it doesn't sound good. We've got to get out of here."

"Wait, what about her?" the other asked but opened the cell without waiting for a response.

Despite verbal abuse and punches and slaps of protest, which barely created a scratch on the man's scarred skin, she was flung over his shoulder, and he walked out of the cell.

"If this place crumbles, she—or rather the thing inside her—is our ticket for survival at Master's hands. You'll thank me later." He walked past the other man, heading toward the only exit from the dungeon.

She couldn't see what was ahead because of the way she was being carried, but she thought they were about halfway through the corridor. The noise in the dungeon suddenly subsided. She couldn't hear the person entering but could tell the power of that person by the pressure in the air and the reaction of the prisoners.

The man carrying her stepped backward slightly.

Then she heard a calm, deep, and powerful male voice. As soon as he spoke, even the insects in the dungeon didn't dare utter a sound.

"Release the prisoners, and I'll let you live."

She didn't know what kinds of creatures the prisoners were, but she recognized their sounds of ultimate joy.

The man holding her captive hesitated then put her down to the floor. While the two men walked past all the cells and opened the doors, she had a full view of the one who had just come to release them all. He looked to be human, in his forties, and incredibly formidable. Although he looked human, the aura around him suggested he was not. Familiar with the house of Gods, she had learned a lot. He didn't have magical energy, but he wasn't human.

When all the released prisoners had exited the dungeon, the man glanced around. Pleased with what he saw, he turned to leave.

The two men who had captured her turned to her. She scooched herself backward on the floor then grabbed a huge piece of dried bone and brandished it at them.

"Don't touch me!" she shouted.

The formidable man stopped at the door of the dungeon. He turned around and came back. He could see now she couldn't walk with her injured leg. He pointed at the man who had carried her before.

"You—take her out of here."

"Who do you think you are? I don't take commands from you," the man said.

"You know who I am. That's why you obeyed me before." He pointed at the other man. "Maybe it's your turn now. You take her. Or maybe I should say whoever takes her out of here will live. If I carry her, I'll have no free hands. You'll attack me. The easiest solution for me is to kill you both and carry her out. But I don't want to kill if it's not necessary."

The second man muttered some profanity but appeared to obey.

Suddenly she was engulfed with a strange muddy smell that seemed to come from nowhere. She felt a presence but couldn't see anything. She pointed the bone at the approaching man.

"No, I can't let them touch me."

Standing at a distance, the man who had carried her before pulled a small knife and stabbed into what appeared to be thin air. A stream of slimy green liquid spurted out, shooting into the face of her savior. He rubbed at his eyes and staggered backward.

The two men charged at him in attack. Their skin glowed in shimmering yellow shades, and they started to change into lizard-like shapes.

Seeing her savior slump to the floor, Charmine held up the bone. "Stop right there. One more step, and I'll curse my own child. You know I'm from the house of Gods. You know if I curse my own child, there will be no cure."

"You won't," a man in half-creature shape growled.

She spoke through her tears. "I have nothing to lose. I'll curse my child and kill myself. Even if your master could retrieve the child from my body, there would be nothing he could do. You know I'm telling the truth."

"She's right," a voice said.

"No, she's bluffing, you idiot."

She raised the bone higher. "In the name of the Gods, in the name of the angels, I, Charmine—"

"No, no, stop! What do you want?"

Before she could answer, her savior darted at them. With two swings of his glowing sword, their two bodies dropped in four pieces on the muddy floor.

He retracted his sword and turned toward her. "Well, I guess I'll have to carry you out of here."

"Thank you for saving my life."

"No, you saved yourself. You're one brave woman. I might have to borrow your eyes—I still can't see anything."

"All right. Over here."

He came to her, groping on the floor. She grabbed his hands to give him guidance. He lifted her up and started walking.

"Straight ahead," she said. "Were did that green poison come from? It seemed to come from nowhere."

The man chuckled. "You obviously don't know where you are. This is Xiilok, the land of multiversal outlaws. This dimension is notorious for its elusive properties. If you're an outsider, you will never see anything real. The creatures with poisonous blood were standing right in front of us, but we couldn't see them." He hit his head on a low-arched door. "Ouch."

"I'm sorry. I meant to say watch your head. That doorway is real."

He shook his head, smiling. "I can see about ten percent now. He glanced down at her face. "You must be good at playing games."

"Why do you say that?"

"That cursing trick can only fool children."

"You think I was bluffing about cursing my child?"

"Curses exist only in fairy tales. Not in my world. I guess if you really believe it, though, I shouldn't call it bluffing. I'm sorry."

She said nothing. This man obviously wasn't from her world. She was wondering, if she went with him to his world, wherever that was, could she erase the curse Luna had put on her child?

"Do you?"

"Huh?"

"Do you believe in miracles?"

"Yes, but it doesn't mean I can do magic. I bluffed the curse on my child when those creatures wanted to attack you. But I don't know magic. My fake curse wouldn't work on my child anyway."

He laughed so heartily that he almost dropped her.

Two men came from around the corner ahead as they approached what appeared to be a hillside.

A man said, "Sciphil Three, we've cleared the right wing . . . Oh . . . are you okay?" His voice trailed off when he saw the green substance and the condition of her savior's eyes.

"I'm fine. Please take my guest to the capsule. Register her to a guest chamber. Be careful, she's injured. I need to wash my eyes."

The man took her. "You let me know if it hurts, ma'am."

"Where are we going?"

"Eudaiz."

"Is that a country?"

"Slightly larger than a country."

"Larger than Earth?"

"It's a universe. Much larger than Earth. But comparison on a physical scale is not accurate. Sciphil Three can explain to you much better than I can."

"What's a sciphil? A guardian angel?"

He laughed. "Yes, that description would work. But the Eudaizian council doesn't approve of magical matters."

"What do you mean?"

"Eudaiz has little tolerance for creatures who call themselves magical—angels, witches, sorcerers. We've had negative experiences with them."

Charmine smiled and nodded, making a mental note not to reveal her true identity to her savior too soon.

CHAPTER 10

Madeline kept her eyes closed but alerted her senses to gather information about the situation. Her mind tracking ability wasn't working right now. She drew in the sense of the room Ciaran had brought her to.

The scent of luxurious wallpaper and scented candle wax hovered in the air. The crackling sound of a fire in a fireplace was gentle, homey, and welcoming. She didn't know who Robert was. Regardless of how enticing the place was and how warm Robert was to her—or rather to Lucy—she didn't belong here. Neither did Ciaran.

Hearing footsteps walking away, she opened one eye and then the other. Dinah was standing right next to her bed, and Arik was peeking outside the room.

"All right, he's away from the corridor," Arik said.

Madeline sat up. "What were the meds you asked Ciaran—"

"Robert," Dinah cut in.

"Well, Ciaran, as Robert, to get for me?"

"I have no idea. Dinah gave me the formula," Arik said.

"It's Iilos's special meat pie. The ingredients are exotic. I'm sure they cannot find them on Earth."

Madeline shook her head. "All right. Now they're trying to make an impossible entree—we can buy some time with that. Can you tell what time period we're in, Arik?"

"I don't know the precise time, but if I'm not mistaken, we're in Abraham Lincoln's time. Robert Lincoln is Abraham Lincoln's eldest son. I recognized the name when he introduced himself." Arik walked around, looking at pictures on the wall to gather as much information as possible.

"The sixteenth president of United States! When you time travel, you land at the time of significant historical events. Is it the Civil War?" Madeline asked.

"That was an important event. But under Lincoln's government, there were many other important events. Any of those could change American history."

Dinah jabbed at her wrist unit. "I'm sorry for my ignorance, and I don't mean to alienate you, but I am kind of an alien here. I don't know American history at all. I'd search my databank, but there's no network available."

"Don't worry, Dinah, we humans should be able to figure out our own history," Arik said.

Madeline paced the room. "What was the most significant event during the Lincoln presidency, apart from the Civil War?"

"Well, it could be we're meant to stop the Civil War. That's what happens every time I travel, right?" Arik raked his hands through his hair.

"We're not supposed to change history. We talked about this, Arik," Madeline said.

Dinah shook her head. "I know you're both concerned about time-traveling rules and principles. But this is an exceptional case. Common time traveling doesn't involve travelers taking roles at the destination without knowing what's going on—like Ciaran is now."

Arik nodded. "And worse, Madeline is supposed to take Lucy's role from Ciaran's—or Robert's—perspective. But she isn't."

"Plus, we're all aware of the situation. But Ciaran isn't," Madeline said. "I think this is another elaborate attempt to manipulate us for the multiversal hologame challenge."

Dinah nodded. "I agree. Do you know who Lucy is, Arik?"

He shook his head. "I'm not a walking, talking history book. Whoever she was, she was involved with Robert in a significant way. The sort of relationship that might create a turn in history."

"How about a significant date? Would that help?" Madeline asked.

Arik nodded.

Dinah rolled her eyes, "Another time and date conversion. I really miss my databank."

"We can use low-tech information, commonly known as a wall calendar, Dinah," Arik said, strolling toward the paper calendar on the wall in the corner of the room.

Madeline followed, frowning at the empty calendar on the wall. "You're saying Robert is Abraham Lincoln's son. So he would take an important role in politics. I've never seen a politician's calendar so clean!"

Arik chuckled. "Maybe it's just a decorative item." Then he continued, "And it's not so clean." He pointed to a needle hole on a date.

"Someone threw a dart at it?" Madeline asked.

Arik nodded. "It's not the throwing but rather the pulling out that I'm more concerned about. There must be a debate, a negotiation, or a consideration of some sort . . . about an action on this particular date."

Dinah cleared her throat. When they turned to face her, they saw her curled comfortably on the reading chair with a soft cashmere throw wrapped around her shoulders.

"May I distract you for just a nanosecond of a multiversal time slot," she asked, "to ask what happened inside Mon Ciel? What caused the one-of-a-kind capsule to explode and shoot through the air? How did we end up transported here, Arik?"

"All I can remember is that Lindsay was either threatened or paid to get the jar of potion I compounded based on Juliette's formula. He called it the primer, I think."

"The primer! Ciaran never mentioned he was looking for the primer inside Mon Ciel!" Dinah exclaimed.

"I don't think he knew what he was after in Juliette's lab," Arik said.

Madeline shook her head. "He knew. He knew it damn well. But he decided not to tell us." She took a deep breath, a technique she often used to staunch unwanted tears.

"Madeline, what's up?" Dinah asked.

"Juliette and Ciaran shared a passion for alchemy and modern chemistry. She developed a primer and was trying to feed it to him—even when she was half dead and universes away. I don't know what the primer was, but even back then, Ciaran was reluctant to talk about it. I think he was afraid of something."

"If *he* was afraid, it must be freaking nasty. Do you know what the primer might be, Dinah?" Arik said.

"Given the situation, I'm guessing the primer is used for multiversal transformation. In a nutshell, it's extremely dangerous and very unpredictable."

"Is it going to explode? Because the last thing I remember is Ciaran holding it in his hand. He might have put it in his pocket," Arik said.

"No, that's not why it's dangerous. The transformative properties must be triggered. If the jar explodes, it won't trigger transformative properties. It will be like an ordinary bomb, like a grenade. That's nothing to Ciaran."

"But he's not Ciaran now. He thinks he's Robert. And God help me if he thinks the jar in his pocket is merely cologne," Arik said.

"Do you know how to trigger the primer, Dinah?" Madeline asked.

"Yes, but I need a lab. And Ciaran's help."

Madeline strode toward the door.

"What are you doing, Madeline?" Arik asked.

"I'm going to find Ciaran and take him back where he belongs."

She exited the room and stared down a long, desolate hallway. She had no clue where Ciaran had gone.

CHAPTER 11

Jael collapsed his wings and glanced around to ensure no creatures had seen him arrive. Xiilok was a place for multiversal outlaws, not angels. His light hair and complexion and his angelic looks made him stick out like a sore thumb. He didn't care to be attacked by Xiilok creatures.

He had been to many places on various missions and had opened his mind to a world of possibilities beyond the world God wanted him to protect. Once he had been out in the multiverse, it was hard to see his missions in the same way.

There were many worlds and different types of creatures who served many Gods. Among those who worshiped no one were Xiilok citizens. They held no religious belief and hence held no moral standards of good or evil. They could kill without worrying that they might upset a superior force.

He arrived at the entrance of a cave and looked up at a magnificent double door in the formation of two stone wings, spreading wide, pointing to the dark sky. He knew the door was an illusion—he saw only what his mind wanted to see. Xiilok citizens could see the real landscape, but all an outsider could do was to try his best not to drop into any oblivion traps.

The winged stone doors opened as he approached. He entered the dark cave, flanked by illuminating bluestone, and arrived at a corner where he found a small residential setting with humble stone furniture.

A man sat on a chair next to a table, focused on a boiling teapot. He greeted Jael without looking up.

"I told you about this day, didn't I, Jael?"

"You summoned me here, Asana."

Asana laughed and turned around. "Your God would summon you. I just called an old friend."

"I am in a difficult situation."

"Yes, I know. But you came when I asked for your help. It's been hundreds of years, and you have never changed."

"What do you need? It sounded urgent."

"I'm sorry about Charmine."

He stared at Asana—his childhood friend was now in the form of a hundred-year-old Xiilok shaman. His appearance had changed greatly, and he had aged a lot. But his sharp eyes were still the same—focused and intense.

"How did you know?"

"A little bird told me a beautiful angel had been captured and was being held in the dungeon of a nearby county."

Jael whirled around. "That's my wife. Where is she?"

Asana shook his head. "I was too late when I came to rescue her. She was captured again by someone else. By the time I called you, they had taken her out of Xiilok."

"She's alive. I can tell."

"Yes, you're right. She's alive because she's carrying a precious piece of property that every creature wants."

"Our child isn't property! I don't have time for this, Asana. What do you want from me?"

"I want to help. I don't know who took her from here, but I know who took her from Earth."

"It's Roallix. I know. So what's the news?"

"He defeated you."

"Roallix beat me once, but only because my guard was down. It won't happen again. Tell me why you want me, or I'm out of here . . . now."

"You let your guard down because you were in love with Charmine. How can you be so sure it won't happen again?"

"It had nothing to do with Charmine. I thought I shouldn't have to protect myself around friends."

"Friends?" Asana laughed. "See what that got you?"

"You're saying I shouldn't trust you as my friend now. I am here for you while my wife is missing. What else do you want from me regarding friendship, Asana?"

Asana stood so tall his head almost hit the ceiling. "You're here because you think you owe me a life. Not because we're friends."

Jael turned around and punched the wall, shaking loose an illuminated candlelit stone and causing it to drop to the ground and shatter.

"We should haven't played that stupid zodiac game. Among the twelve of us, only you made it. Now Roallix has turned dark, and Arete is a lost cause."

Jael raised a hand, stopping Asana from speaking. "What's your point?"

Asana glanced at the teapot to be sure it wasn't boiling over. "You owe me nothing, Jael. I pushed you through the rainbow of light because I believed you could make it. I—and others—weren't going to make it. I hoped when you became an angel, you'd help us. And you did. You gave me another life—a second chance here. So I'll return the favor now."

Asana removed the teapot from the fire and poured it into a jar of potion. The liquid bubbled up a bit and then simmered down into a liquid of a light golden color. He gave it to Jael.

Jael raised an eyebrow. "A healing compound?" he asked.

"You could say so. It's a compound that helps creatures move between worlds and transform without harm. Especially for those with . . . a traveler's spirit." Asana lowered his voice as he said it.

Jael's eyes darkened.

Asana stepped back and continued. "I know about Charmine's origins. I know you smuggled her into the world of the Gods without jumping through the light the way you did. And because of that, she never properly transformed. She wasn't made for being an angel." Before Jael could react, Asana raised a hand to stop him. "I told you, I am your friend—perhaps the one and only in this multiverse.

The fact that I knew and did nothing proves my friendship and my loyalty to you. Your secret is safe with me."

Jael calmed down and nodded. "So I do owe you." Jael raised the jar of potion to the level of his eyes and looked at the still-warm liquid. "But how does this potion help Charmine?"

"I thought about this when I heard she had been taken out of Xiilok via the Daimon Gate. Only privileged member universes have access to the Daimon Gate. I'm sure you know this. So that means she has been transported out of the magical world of the Gods."

"So if she survives being transported out of the magical world, taking your potion would help me to bring her back properly?"

Asana smiled. "Yes, and then she can be properly transformed into an angel."

"What's in this for you, Asana?"

Asana sat down on an illuminated stone bench. "My time is almost up. After I die, I'd like you to take me back to Earth, burn my body, and let my ashes scatter in the wind in the place where we played the zodiac game."

"I can take you back right now so that you can live on Earth."

"What year is it now on Earth?"

"1864." Jael shook his head. "I'm sorry for my ignorance. You are long past the normal human lifespan."

Asana shrugged. "I like it here. I'm useful as a shaman. You should go now. There are many thousands of member universes of the Daimon Gate. It will take time to find out which one Charmine has been taken to."

He stood and saw Jael to the door.

Asana came back inside. He sat down and stared for a long time at a large stone vase in the corner. Then he opened the lid of the vase. When a colorful snake rose up from it, he grabbed its neck and took it to the fireplace where he had made the potion before and placed it in the pot.

A short moment later, the snake slithered away, vanishing through a gap at the base of the stone wall.

CHAPTER 12

Arik felt them coming—the incredible and uncontrollable heat waves that burned his body and mind. There was nothing he could do about it. He knew he would lose consciousness soon. He braced his hands on the wall next to the calendar he was examining, and he saw a blurry date going in and out of focus—1864.

The calendar and the date glared at him, zooming in and out as if in an extremely fast sequence of camera snaps. He could hear his heart rate intensifying, beating in tune with the clock ticking on the wall, and feel the sweat trickling down his forehead.

"Arik, are you okay?"

He wanted to respond, but no words came out of his mouth. It felt as if thousands of needles were jabbing at his brain. He was breathless with the sensation. Arik shook his head.

"Look at me, Arik, please."

He grabbed his head and felt a strong pull to fly—he knew it was the urge to travel back to 2017. The same sensation had occurred every time he was pulled to travel to the past, but never on the return trip. The returns were always instant, smooth, and fast.

Still, whichever way it went, he had no control over this process. He had the daunting feeling that if he resisted this pull, his head was going to explode. He felt to the floor.

"You're heating up. Tell me what's happening, Arik."

He felt Dinah's hands grabbing his.

"I'm returning . . . leaving . . ."

"No, you can't. You'll leave Madeline and Ciaran here. You're the vessel. You transported them here, and you have to bring them back."

"I . . . I can't control it . . ."

"You can. Just open your eyes and look at me."

He tried and saw a blast of bright light that shocked his system. "I can't see a thing . . . My head is going to explode . . ."

"It will if you let it, Arik. You have to take control of your mind. You have to tell it how you want it to work. It's your mind, for pity's sake."

"I can't . . ."

He felt her hands pinning his to the floor.

"It's *your* mind. *You* control it. No creature in the multiverse has the right to manipulate anyone's mind without consent. And you didn't consent to any of this."

"I don't know what I did or didn't do anymore." The pain was unbearable. It felt as if his brain was squeezing itself out of this skull.

"You're a very strong human, Arik. Don't let anything from the multiverse control you."

"I can't help it."

"Now Arik, I want you to open your eyes and see my face. You have to want to see me to do it. Your vision is your first sense, and you are in control of it. Don't just accept whatever comes at you. You have to want to see me, and only me."

Her voice was soothing but determined. It was as strong as the force that was pulling at him. The pain subsided slightly. He opened his eyes, willing his mind's eye to see Dinah.

There she was. Big, beautiful eyes, dark and full of secrets. Pouting lips that always made him want to taste them. He was sure they would be as sweet as the lilting voice that made her sounded like an Irish lullaby whenever she spoke.

She smiled. "Hello there! What are you seeing?"

"Beauty."

"Beauty is in the eye of the beholder. Isn't that a common saying on Earth? You see, you can do it."

Before he could respond, her image vanished, and the pain hit him as fast and strong as an explosion. He was drifting. He heard Dinah's voice from a distance.

"Can you hear me, Arik?"

"Yes . . ." He pounded his head on the floor.

"You'll need some help to stay. Do you want to stay here for your friends?"

"Yes . . . but I can't control it." He pounded his head again.

"Don't do it, Arik. I'll help you. But there will be risks."

"If I die, so be it."

"No, death is the easy part, Arik. It's your mind we will be working with. It might change you."

"Okay, fine, I'll take the chance. But you have to promise me one thing."

"What?"

"If I'm out of control . . . in a bad way . . . put a bullet in my head."

"Arik!"

"Promise?"

"Fine. I promise. Now can we go ahead and do this? You're blanking out so quickly."

He nodded.

"All right, I'm going to inject you with a formula I developed. You'll feel a new sensation. Whatever direction the new sensation pulls you, follow it. Open your mind, relax, follow it, and you'll be fine. Got it?"

He nodded again. He felt the prick of a needle on his neck at the jugular, and waves of coolness followed. He did what he was told. He emptied his mind, drained it of all the worries and burdens of earthly matters.

He waited.

Then the new sensation came. The surge of energy was overwhelmingly powerful. It filled his mind. Every cell in his body was bursting with the life force. It flowed in and out. In and out. The flow inside him stopped, creating a suction. His energy was strained, tense as a taut bow.

An incredible urge to connect with and exchange energy washed over him. And he responded.

He felt the cold floor, warm flesh, and soft fabric. He tasted the sweetness of feminine skin and the saltiness of sweat and tears. He smelled the tanginess of sexuality.

His mind floated. His body erupted with urges to take, give, and pass on energy like a conduit. He needed to connect. And he did just that until the sensation was sated.

Then he was drowsy. Calmness descended on him.

After a while, he opened his eyes. His mind was crystal clear. He was fully aware of his surroundings.

Now he was in control of his mind and his body as Dinah had said he would be. *Where's Dinah?* he thought and sat up quickly from the floor.

He looked down at his completely naked body.

He grabbed his pants which were in a crumpled heap on the floor nearby and slid them on. He scrambled up to his feet and saw Dinah sitting on the sofa, looking at him with a smile on her face.

She was fully dressed, but her hair was tousled, her lips were slightly swollen, and the top button of her blouse was undone.

Arik looked down at his body then back at Dinah. Her smile continued.

He prowled around the room, then came back, crouching in front of the sofa. He remembered the strong force of the activity, whatever it was. He remembered his hands pressing hard into fragile skin. And he remembered the salty taste of sweat. And unmistakably, he remembered the taste of tears.

He rubbed his thumb at the corner of her eye where there was still a trace of a teardrop. "Did I hurt you?"

"No." She jerked her face away from his hand.

He backed away and stood up. "Did we make love?"

She smiled again then leaned back into the sofa, buttoned up her blouse, and looked him in the eye.

"No, we didn't make love. We had sex."

CHAPTER 13

At the end of the corridor, Madeline approached a door. She could hear Robert's voice from within. "I told you, they're Lucy's friends. They're fine."

"Good friends would not drag you into the woods for two days and make you stand in for a play!"

"They don't know I'm against theater, Sam."

"You're not against theater. You just want to protect your father's political career. John is a danger you have to eliminate."

"I'm a lawyer, not a politician. And eliminating an opponent doesn't have to mean murder."

"Since when did you go soft?"

"Don't judge me, Sam."

"I'm not judging. You'll never get over Lucy, will you? Oh, for pity's sake, she rejected you twice, and you're still being noble?"

"This has nothing to do with Lucy. I'm not killing anyone on a hunch."

"Robert, you always have good instincts, and you're a great judge of character. Tonight's rehearsal is your one and only chance to kill him. We've been working on this for weeks—"

"Yes, and we haven't reached a definite decision. If I had enough evidence, I wouldn't hesitate to kill him. But we don't. If you can get this medicine for Lucy, it will be greatly appreciated."

Madeline sneaked closer to the door so she could hear the conversation clearer.

"I told you, John Wilkes Booth isn't just an ordinary actor. You know he's up to something. You'll regret it if you don't kill him tonight, Robert."

"Where is the medicine Arik gave me?"

"Hey, are you listening to me? What are you looking for?"

"A piece of paper. Arik gave me the prescribed medicine for Madeline."

"Who's Madeline?"

"What?"

"You just said Madeline."

116

"I don't know anyone with that name. I can't find the damn piece of paper. I—"

"Come on, do you hear me, Robert? We've planned tonight's kill for many weeks. You vanished for two days, came back with Lucy and her friends, and totally changed your mind. I thought the fact that Lucy showed affection for John would give you stronger motivation."

"This has nothing to do with that. She's a free woman. She can have a romance with whoever she wants. Where is that piece of paper?"

"What drugs are you looking for?"

"I'm not a doctor. How should I know?"

There was a clank sound as if a hard object was slammed on a wooden table.

"What is this?" Sam asked. "It smells like cheap perfume."

"I don't know. Just found it in my pocket now. I have to go back to ask Arik again for the medicine. You can keep the perfume!"

Madeline rushed into the room and smiled as graciously as she could.

"Lucy? Are you okay? I was just trying to get you the medicine. You scared the hell out of me!" Ciaran as Robert said, rushing over to her side.

"Yes, I'm fine. Thank you for bringing me here. Dinah told me. I wouldn't care for being taken home." She looked at Sam. "There's no need to get the medicine for me. By the way, the perfume is mine, Sam, can I please have it back?"

Sam frowned then gave her the jar of potion Madeline knew was the primer Ciaran had taken from Mon Ciel.

"Thank you. Arik and Dinah want to talk to you about the play. They have some important information for you, Robert," Madeline said.

"All right," Ciaran said and was about to follow Madeline out of the room.

"Robert, we have to agree on this first," Sam growled.

"It can wait."

"No."

Ciaran turned toward Madeline. "I'll be there to talk to Arik and Dinah shortly, Lucy."

Madeline nodded and reluctantly left the room.

She scurried back to the room where Arik and Dinah were. As she pushed the door open, she saw Arik standing topless in the middle of the room. Dinah sat on a reading chair. Madeline smelled the faint scent of sex in the air.

"What happened?" she asked.

Arik tossed his shirt on. "Nothing, according to Dinah," Arik muttered.

"I didn't say it was nothing. I said you had an inaccurate understanding of the activity," Dinah said.

"What activity?" Madeline asked.

"Never mind," Arik murmured.

Dinah smiled. "He almost traveled back to the current time without you and Ciaran. But we have it under control now. Still, we'd better get Ciaran back here and stay in close proximity in case Arik has the urge to travel again."

"You're saying after all we went through, my control won't last?" Arik exclaimed.

"People are different, Arik. You might be at the tail end of the population. We're better safe than sorry. And for your information, nothing lasts forever."

"What population? You've never tested your drug on anyone before?"

Dinah had her hands on her hips. "You agreed to it. I just wanted to help. I did test the drug, though."

"On space creature?"

"No, on a pig."

Arik turned around, staring at the wall as if he could eat it alive.

"Okay, that's enough you two," Madeline said. "I'll get Ciaran and come back. Here's the primer." She put the jar on the table.

Dinah rushed over. She picked the jar up and stared at the liquid inside. "Magnificent piece of work!" she said.

At the doorway, Madeline turned back and said, "Sam and Robert were planning to kill someone named John Wilkes Booth. Does that ring any bells, Arik?"

Arik's eyes darkened. "Are you sure?"

"Positive. He repeated it several times. It seems there's a love triangle going on between Lucy, John, and Robert. I think John might be winning."

"John Wilkes Booth assassinated Abraham Lincoln," Arik said as he strolled toward the door.

"So the assassination is the significant event we're meant to fix? We have to stop Robert from killing his father's assassin and let his father be killed later? What kind of twisted joke is this?" Madeline said, trailing behind Arik.

"Welcome to the club, Madeline. It's not the first time I've had that kind of thought about twisted fate," Arik said.

Dinah followed Arik and Madeline.

The trio charged down the corridor and stormed into the room where Robert and Sam were, only to find an empty room.

"If Robert kills John Wilkes Booth, Abraham Lincoln will survive that event, and that will change American history," Arik said.

CHAPTER 14

Charmine clutched at her stomach as the pain intensified. Sweat streamed down her forehead. Her vision blurred with the agony. She hadn't been settled in Eudaiz long enough to know her way around. Everything in this place was different from her world. The chamber was small, the walls were like stone but felt as cool as metal. She reached up from the chair she was sitting on and braced her hands on the wall, finding the cool temperature helped ease her pain.

"You are in discomfort and your body temperature is one hundred percent higher than normal. Please place your palm on the control panel for further diagnosis," said a monotone female voice coming from a smooth rectangular surface on the wall.

She was startled and pushed back hard from the wall. She was off balance, and the chair tipped over, dropping her to the floor.

"Dear guest SCP3, please place your palm on the control panel for further diagnosis. Preliminary calculation suggests there is a high probability you will require medical assistance."

The thing that looked like a mirror was talking to her!

Although she was in agony, she was sure only the Winter Queen in a fairy tale she had grown up reading would talk to a mirror on the wall. With the pain in her tummy and the slowly healing wounds on her savaged leg, she didn't need a mirror to tell her she needed help.

She loved fairy tales, but talking to a mirror was neither magical nor practical right now. She shook her head to rid herself of the idea of having a conversation with an inanimate object.

"Please verify your palm on the control panel immediately. Your medical issue has a high possibility of being terminal."

She was on the verge of passing out because of the pain. In Scotland, when her vicious evil sister had twisted her leg and broken it, she'd thought that was the most excruciating pain she had ever experienced.

She was wrong.

The pain she was experiencing right now was much worse. If she died here, she would never get to see Jael again. What about their child?

"Where is the panel?" she asked and wasn't surprised to hear the mirror respond.

"Please follow the light," it said.

A rectangular green light appeared on the shiny surface of the mirror. She braced herself, stood up, and was about to place her palm on the panel. Then she stopped. "What sort of information will you need for your diagnosis?"

The monotone voice responded, "All pertinent medical data to benchmark against our healthy Eudaizian model."

"How detailed?"

"Basic details about your make, your history, cosmos origin—"

"No," she muttered and put her palm down. Then the pain hit her again like a storm. She fell to the floor and almost passed out.

She would rather die than have her origin exposed.

She needed to leave here. She tried to stand up with her one good leg, but she failed and flopped to the floor.

The steel door of the chamber slid open, and Sciphil Three rushed in. "I heard the report and the warning signals about your condition," he said calmly and put her back on the chair. "I'm sorry I left you alone in the guest chamber. I should have assigned medical staff."

"Did that mirror tell you?"

He smiled a kindhearted, honest smile, and if she weren't committed to someone already, she thought she may have fallen for that. "Not a mirror. They call it a computer here. Its abilities are a lot more sophisticated than mere reflection. Do you mind if I place your palm on the panel for further diagnosis? The wounds on your leg are taking longer to heal than I anticipated. I don't understand how it could cause you such pain."

"It's because I didn't let you use your preferred treatment method."

"You must have your reasons for deciding not to receive treatments. I won't press for information you don't want to give. But the computer diagnosis suggests that your health is deteriorating. I can assure you the tests are not invasive."

She shook her head.

Her vision started to blur, and she could feel herself passing away. Then she felt a lift. Sciphil Three had forced her palm onto the shiny surface of the panel.

The computer streamed out lines of text that she couldn't understand.

Sciphil Three put her back down in the chair and saw the tears gleaming in her eyes.

"I apologize for doing this to you. But I can't let you die without knowing why." He turned and glanced at the computer's results. Then his deep, dark gray eyes returned to her teary face.

"I'm a traveler. Please don't tell . . ." Exhausted and plagued with agony, she cried.

He crouched in front of her chair. "I don't care if you're a gypsy of the multiverse. My concern is that you are pregnant. I brought you here without knowing. In Eudaiz, the gestation terms are calculated by days. The child has to be taken out of the mother's body on day three, or the mother will die in agony, and the child will perish."

"What do you mean by taken out?"

"The child is removed from the mother's body via a delicate procedure and supported by our system until the child is strong enough to return to the mother. The process is pain-free, and the success rate is ninety-nine percent if conducted in time."

"Am I too late?"

He nodded. "I have not seen a case of survival at this late stage." He looked into her eyes. "Any ordinary creature would have died already. You should have died instantly the moment I took you into this dimension. I should have been more careful."

"It's a miracle."

He shook his head. "I don't think so. But I didn't take you out of Xiilok to see you die in Eudaiz—the justice system in this multiverse be damned."

"There is no justice even in the house of Gods!"

Sciphil Three held her right hand and snapped a square pad on her wrist. The pain subsided instantly. "I apologize again. This is the treatment you have been refusing. Being a traveler will get you killed in the wider multiverse, but I assure you, that will not happen in my universe. We don't discriminate."

"How can you be so sure?"

"There is nothing I can say with certainty. But I will find a way to save you and your child."

She shook her head. Now that the pain had turned into a mist, her mind started to clear. This was the first time she'd been able to take a good look at Sciphil Three—strong, masculine face, striking gray eyes, dark hair, and the body of a warrior. He looked as young as Jael. But while Jael had an angelic gleam of light around him, Sciphil Three had an authoritative aura—one she could tell made people want to obey him.

"My origin wasn't the only issue that held me back from receiving treatments. I know you don't believe in magic, and Eudaiz doesn't support magical creatures, but my child was cursed. I need to find my husband. He knows how to deal with this problem. I won't let my child come into any world carrying a curse."

Sciphil Three stared at her for a brief second as if he didn't know what to say. Then he nodded. "So it's not just a matter of belief. You come from the magical world—a dimension I am always reluctant to interact with."

"A dimension?"

"Never mind. What does your husband do?"

She smiled to prepare him for the answer. "He's the angel of light."

Sciphil Three nodded. "I understand. You need to find your husband and then decide what to do with the child. I can't help much when it comes to magic. But your painkiller will wear off very soon. I need to make sure I can take you out of Eudaiz safely."

"Eudaiz is governed the way it is for a reason. I don't want you harmed for breaking the rules."

He let out a hearty laugh. "Sciphil Three is the king Sciphil. In that regard, I believe I have some protection. Rules are created by the council, and I am the head of the council. I'll find a way out for you."

"What's a sciphil?"

"It is an abbreviated form of Scientist Philosopher. I lean toward the first word. But I'll need to use the second to understand where you come from. Time is running out. I should go. Please stay inside the chamber. Don't let anyone in, don't follow anyone out, and don't follow anyone's instructions."

She smiled. "I'll try not to die on you. I don't know anything about kingship, but I'm sure this will put you in more danger than you think. Please be careful."

"Thank you. I'll be careful." He paused and looked into her eyes. "I didn't know being cared for could feel so pleasant." He nodded a goodbye and turned around.

"Does the king have a name?"

"Malachi LeBlanc." He smiled and exited the door.

Charmine stared at the closed steel door for a long time. Her smile had faded. She hated herself right now.

She hadn't learned much from her gypsy tribe before she left them. But there was one set of skills she took with her—she could see dark energy from a demon before it took possession of a soul near death.

And she had seen it all over Malachi just before he left the chamber.

CHAPTER 15

In a small alley leading toward the back of the theater, Madeline glanced back to ensure that Arik and Dinah still trailed behind her. The year 1864 hadn't been kind to any of them. Arik and Dinah had no tech and nobody to support them. So Madeline had to rely solely on her mind tracking ability, which had decided to work on a patchy basis, turning itself on and off whenever it pleased.

The street was crowded with flocks of merchants, carriages, and people rushing around resuming their usual daily activities after a heavy thunderstorm. As soon as the storm concluded, people began to move around, trying to catch up on what they had lost during the poor weather.

"It's a very busy theater, Madeline. I wouldn't plan to kill anyone here," Arik said.

"I saw the address in Sam's mind when he gave me the primer potion. My mind tracking is very consistent when it comes to him. I can't see Ciaran's at all, but the tracking signal for Sam is crystal clear."

"I wonder why. He's a total stranger," Dinah asked.

Madeline shook her head. She didn't want to be distracted from the trail as she might lose it at any point. They needed to get to the theater and stop Robert from killing John.

She had no idea how things would turn out, nor did she have any plan of how to stop the killing. *Some sparks of precognition would help!* she thought, but knowing her mind, she stopped wasting her energy hoping.

"As soon as you see Ciaran, try to grab him and get him close to us. I'll see if we can transport back to our time," Arik said.

"But I thought you couldn't control either coming here or leaving . . ." Madeline trailed off. "Or can you now?"

Arik glanced back quickly at Dinah, who stood behind Madeline and said nothing. "Dinah tested a drug on me. It's supposed to help me control the entry and exit points of time traveling. I don't know if it'll work now, but it worked before. It stopped me from involuntarily going back to 2017. I think if I could resist that travel, I should be able to initiate it now. I'm working on it. So try to stay close in case I need to grab you all."

"Understood," Madeline said as she found an entrance to the backstage of the theater and entered it. It was a narrow pathway flanked by black fabric that covered large boxes, tools, and stage equipment. Unlike the streets, which were buzzing with activity, the backstage was quiet.

The air was so still Madeline heard herself breathing. Then it dawned on her that her mind had gone quiet. She had lost track of Sam's mind. She had no clue where he and Robert were. Arik and Dinah still trailed behind her.

Then she heard the faint sounds of a conversation. She recognized Robert and Sam's voices, and she heard another male voice.

"Okay, we can hear them. When we get to them, I'll talk Ciaran out of this killing and off the stage, and then you give me a signal to let me know if you can initiate travel. How does that sound, Arik?"

"My suggestion is for me to shoot sedative needles in both Ciaran and John. Then we can grab Ciaran," Dinah said.

"That's a very good suggestion, Dinah. I had totally forgotten about your sneaky weapon," Madeline said.

They heard the loud report of a gunshot.

"This is not good. Change of plans. You needle all of them when we get there, Dinah," Madeline said. "Please see if you can initiate travel now, Arik."

"I'm on it."

They charged in the direction of the gunshot.

Approaching from the side of the stage, Madeline could see Ciaran and a man pointing guns at each other. The other man had his back to Madeline. Next to Ciaran, Sam's body lay on the stage floor, blood pooling around him. Ciaran's eyes were bloodshot, and she knew that no matter what form he was in, Robert or Ciaran, he was in a rage, and he would kill.

She didn't want to call out to distract Ciaran, so she kept hurrying toward the stage. When the other man heard footsteps behind him, he turned and copped Dinah's needle to the chest.

Madeline charged past the man as he fell down to the stage floor into a coma induced by Dinah's needle. She ran toward Ciaran.

"Don't come near me, Lucy," Robert yelled and waved the gun.

From behind her, she heard Arik yell, "This isn't John."

She turned around, immediately registering the situation. Robert and Sam had been facing two gunmen from the side of the stage. The one who'd gunned down Sam and copped Dinah's needle wasn't Booth. However, the man she could now see standing on the other side of a stage curtain, pointing a gun at Robert, was none other than the sinfully handsome stage performer, John Wilkes Booth. He looked at her with eyes determined to kill.

To wave Lucy out of the way, Robert had moved his gun away from the aim he had held on John. The position in which John was standing made it impossible for Dinah to shoot a needle. Robert was worried that Lucy was in the crossfire, and John didn't look hesitant to shoot.

The precognition Madeline had had before this trip that Ciaran would be killed with a knife wound to the chest made perfect sense now, except it wasn't a combat knife but a gun—a more efficient and lethal weapon.

Dinah was in a position to shoot a needle at Ciaran, which would take him down and thus out of the line of the coming bullet should John fire. All Madeline needed to do was to signal Dinah. But the whole thing was speculation on her part. If her plan didn't work, and it didn't remove Ciaran from the line of fire, that would mean Dinah's needle would incapacitate Ciaran and possibly get him killed.

She decided not to signal Dinah. She looked at John and could see in his eyes that he was going to pull the trigger. His gun was pointed toward Ciaran and her. If Lucy had rejected Robert because of John Wilkes Booth, what was happening now suggested that she had never meant anything to John.

"Get out of the way, Lucy." Robert waved his gun frantically, disregarding the danger coming his way.

John Wilkes Booth pulled the trigger.

Madeline switched on her supernatural power and could see the bullet moving through the air as if in slow motion.

She stepped into the path of the flying bullet.

In the back of her mind, she heard Arik and Dinah talking, or maybe shouting. It happened so fast she didn't have time to think of anything else or summon her unstable precognitive vision.

Then everything went black.

CHAPTER 16

Jael cringed at the impact of the explosion and hoped the giant silver egg that had just exploded in the air didn't carry the person who had sent him the message asking to meet at the multiversal transitional zone. After the dust of the explosion settled, a tall and formidable man emerged from behind a large shard of stone and walked toward him.

Jael straightened his posture in anticipation of a possible attack. He shouldn't be in the transitional zone of the multiverse where magical creatures like him were most vulnerable. In other worlds, there were advanced civilizations with knowledge and technology he would never be able to access as a magical creature. His God and fellow angels were in worse situations because they couldn't even grasp the concept of technology.

But the message was about his wife, and for that, he was willing to take any risks.

"It's a pleasure to meet you in person, Jael." The man pointed at the dust remnants from the explosion hovering in the air. "That's just a setup."

"How do I address you?"

"Who I am is not important. But it is critical that I can verify you are who you say you are. This is the transitional zone, and Xiilok creatures are notorious for their ability to disguise."

"Then how do I know you're not a Xiilok creature in disguise?"

The man chuckled. "Well said. All right. I sent Jael a message about a lady who travels a lot. If you are he, you will know what I'm talking about."

Jael shrugged. "I know what you're talking about. But how do I prove I know without exposing an important piece of information to the wrong person?"

The man nodded. "Prove to me you are an angel. That's not a secret and certainly not sensitive information."

Jael stepped back, spread his wings, and shot up into the air. He flew around, came back, and landed. No creature could fake his angel wings and the light emanating from the tip of every feather.

He wasn't sure who Charmine's savior was. But for that man to take her out of Xiilok safely and track him down, Jael knew he wasn't an ordinary citizen of the multiverse. He needed to impress this man to get his wife back. If he was a Xiilok creature, then seeing Jael in full angel form would intimidate him and stop him from doing whatever he had intended to do.

"I believe Xiilok creatures can fly like that, and they can glow like candles, too. They're not difficult tricks," the man deadpanned.

"I don't do tricks!" Jael shouted. He was so angry that he was sure his wings would spontaneously spread again.

Then the man smiled. "You're really Jael, Charmine's husband. Based on the information she gave me, I figured there was a big chance you'd react the way you just did."

"So you're what, a wizard?"

"No, in my world, what I just did is called psychological profiling. I'm quite good at it."

"Are you two finished grilling each other?"

It was Charmine's voice. Jael's senses perked up. He literally sniffed the air for a trace of her scent and darted toward the rocks.

There she was, his wife, as beautiful as ever, sitting on the grass and leaning against a rock. He rushed over and pulled her into his arms. He craved the feel of her body, the scent of her skin, the gleam of joy in her eyes whenever she looked at him.

His wife was alive.

She traced her hand along his shoulders where the old wings would have been before Luna, her evil sister, and her people savaged his angel wings and his power.

"It didn't hurt. And it's healed," he said. "I have new wings now."

Then his eyes landed on her injured leg.

"It didn't hurt, either. And it's healed," she said. Then she kissed him.

"Are you two finished grilling each other?" said Malachi LeBlanc, sitting on top of the rock, looking down at them. "I don't mean to be rude, but we are in the transitional zone of the multiverse, and anything can happen here. Also, I've just faked her death in the explosion. I need to go back to

Eudaiz to receive the report about the incident and pretend to be surprised by the news."

Charmine smiled. "This is Sciphil Three of Eudaiz. He saved our child and me," she said.

Jael turned around. He could hear the rumbling of gossip among creatures across the multiverse. But now, seeing for himself, the multiverse had it all wrong.

Sciphil Three of Eudaiz didn't have a dragon's head, wasn't ten feet tall, didn't look as if he could spread a twenty-foot wingspan and spit out toxic fireballs.

This was no more than a powerful and formidable man in his late thirties, or early forties. Most importantly, he used to be human.

"You're the king Sciphil of Eudaiz," Jael said.

"You're quite knowledgeable, Jael. Yes, I am king. But it doesn't mean I'm invincible. And if you expected me to have two dragon heads, I'm sorry to disappoint. I have one head, and it could be quite vulnerable in this transitional zone."

"Understood. We should get going. Thank you for taking care of Charmine."

Sciphil Three nodded and descended from the rock. "Charmine will fill you in later on the information about her pregnancy and the implications of entering Eudaiz. The short version of the solution I can give you now is this." Sciphil Three pulled out two bracelets from his pocket and gave them to Jael and Charmine.

"Jael, I know you travel a lot, and you take Charmine with you wherever you go. It might have been fine before because you have been traveling within the magical world. But now that she has entered Eudaiz, her profile is in the multiversal databank. She has been materialized and can be tracked."

Jael raked his hands through his hair. "I should have anticipated that if I kept taking her with me, she would cross worlds one day."

"I think a quick 101 lesson about different worlds might be helpful!" Charmine arched an eyebrow.

Malachi smiled patiently. "In principle, there are three worlds—the magical world, the material world, and Amalgam, the ever-changing world in between."

Jael said, "Angels and magical creatures live in the magical world. A large part of the multiverse, including Earth, your favorite holiday destination, belongs to the material world. Generally, ordinary creatures cannot cross worlds."

"But we've been to Earth!" Charmine said.

"We never participated in that world as living entities. We just visited. I used to be human. But once I crossed to the magical world a long time ago, I became a magical creature forever," Jael said.

"How did you cross, may I ask?" Malachi said.

"Twelve of us were playing a stupid zodiac game in the middle of a stormy night. We saw a light in the sky like a rainbow, and we jumped through it. How about you? I'm guessing you used to be human."

Malachi shrugged, "Inheritance of a troubled bloodline."

"The LeBlancs?" Charmine asked.

Malachi chuckled. "Very few creatures in the multiverse know my name. Let's keep it that way. Anyway, the bracelets you have now are Iilos technology. If you wear the bracelets, you will be able to lock in your profile, regardless of which worlds you travel to. And you will be like that forever. That's the simplest way I can put it."

"Immortality?" Charmine asked.

Malachi winced. "That's highly debatable. Let's leave it for another time. But for now, the practical issue is that once you lock in or trigger it, you have to wear it forever. If you take it off, you will be reversed to the original form exponentially, accumulating the time and space effect. In a word, it's ugly."

"We'll think carefully before using it," Jael said.

"The other issue is about her pregnancy. If she weren't a traveler, she would have been dead when I took her into Eudaiz. But still, the system in Eudaiz has registered her, so sooner or later—"

"It might not be an issue anymore," Jael said.

"How so?"

"My friend is a shaman, and he gave me a potion that will help Charmine transform properly into a magical creature. Then I will take her back to the house of Gods for protection."

"May I see the potion?" Malachi asked and reached his hand out.

"Why?"

"I just want to see what's in it."

Jael frowned but then obeyed.

Malachi looked at the jar carefully then said, "I'm going to scan it. I won't need to take a sample. I just want to make sure the ingredients inside have no conflicting properties with the pain relief patch I have given Charmine."

Jael nodded.

"No," Charmine said.

"Why not?" Malachi asked.

"I see dark energy from the demon all over you. That energy always covers a near dead soul. I know you don't believe in this. But I'm a traveler, and that's one of my talents."

Malachi smiled. "Thank you for your concern. But I'm not going to take this potion. I won't even touch it. I just need to scan for its properties." He flicked the lid open and hovered his wrist unit quickly over the top.

The unit flashed a green light and let out a happy ping.

Malachi smiled. "You see. It's harmless."

Suddenly, a colorful snake shot up in the air from the grass and bit Malachi's hand. He dropped the potion to the ground, and the liquid spilled and steamed up. He grabbed his wrist with the other hand. "It's not poisonous," he said, but his words trailed off quickly, and he slumped to the ground.

The snake dropped back to the ground and slithered away.

Jael darted over, picked the jar of potion up, and threw it away. But Malachi had inhaled the steam. "Goddamn you, Asana!" Jael roared in anger.

Charmine tore off the hem of her dress and tied it around Malachi's upper arm. Her voice was shaky. "Jael, he's leaving us . . . Jael, please do something . . ."

Jael darted over and held Malachi's hands. "The steam of the potion combined with the snake venom makes the most toxic compound in the magical world. It can kill angels. Tell me Sciphil Three of Eudaiz, if I take you back to your universe, can your technology save you?"

There was no response from Malachi. Jael streamed light into Malachi via their connected hands. Malachi stirred. Jael knew his energy wouldn't last long. As soon as Malachi opened his eyes, he repeated the question.

"Yes," Malachi said weakly. "But to take me back to Eudaiz, you both have to wear the bracelets."

CHAPTER 17

Dinah coughed out the wet grass, leaves, and dirt she had unintentionally swallowed when she landed roughly on the ground.

"Damn it! A soft landing would've been nice, Arik."

She propped herself up on her elbows then scrambled to her feet. She didn't recognize her surroundings and didn't know where they were, but she was sure it wasn't the creek down the hill at Henley-on-Thames, where they'd departed.

She seemed to be standing on soft grass. Judging by the slope of the ground, they might have landed on a hillside. The fog surrounding them was so thick she could barely see Ciaran and Madeline, who were sitting up about ten feet away. They looked around, getting their bearings. They looked to be alive, for now, so she turned to look for Arik.

Arik pulled himself up from the ground and glanced around groggily. Dinah knew he lost memories and was always disoriented after time traveling, but she had never before seen him in such poor condition. His eyes were bloodshot, and blood trickled from his nose and over his lips.

She rushed over, brushing a stray hair from his forehead. "You okay? Tell me you're fine, Arik."

He nodded.

She wiped the blood off his face and helped him stand. He swayed, towering over her. "All right, easy, easy. Why don't you just lie down for a bit?" She eased him back down to the ground.

"I'm fine. It was just a hard bump." He tried to sit up, but she gently pushed him down again.

Ciaran stood up and rushed toward his wife. "Are you okay, Madeline?" he asked. "I thought we fell into the water at the creek. Why aren't we wet?"

Dinah smiled down at Arik. "It looks like our Ciaran is missing a chapter!"

"It's about damn time he missed something," Arik muttered.

Dinah grinned. "I don't know where or when we are now, but if you remember what happened just before this, you're one up on Ciaran," she said.

"I have no desire to even the score with him."

"All right, but do you remember?"

"Yes."

"Really? What do you remember?"

"Okay, it was 1864, Abraham Lincoln's time. John Wilkes Booth was about to shoot Ciaran, thinking he was Robert Lincoln, Abraham Lincoln's eldest son. Madeline was thought to be Lucy Hale, maybe the love interest of both John *and* Robert. But our Madeline's mind wasn't affected the way Ciaran's was, so she was well aware of the situation. Her ingenious solution was to jump into the crossfire to cop the bullet. That forced me to initiate my time travel to save the day. I jumped in, grabbing them both before the bullet hit Madeline. How do I score on this history test?"

She grinned. "You are now able to activate your time travel—and remember what happened afterward. You seem to be in total control of your mind now. Pertaining to the time traveling, I mean. So what we did before has at least some benefit."

"Benefit? You know what, Dinah? Things might be different in your universe, but in this world, when you combine sexual activity with benefit, it's called prostitution. You're making me feel like a male whore."

He sat up and stared straight into her eyes. His soft green eyes grew intense and made her stomach quiver. Then he got to his feet and walked toward Madeline and Ciaran.

She frowned. *What did he just say? A* male *whore?* But before she could ponder any further, her wrist unit emitted a happy ping. "Great, my technology is back. Thank the multiversal god of technology!" she muttered, wondering if there was such a god. She turned around to talk to Ciaran, but before she could say a word, the hill shook with the impact of what felt like an explosion, throwing everyone to the ground.

Dinah planted her face in the grass again, lying still for a moment before jumping back up to her feet.

"That's them! They're the ones who bumped us down here!" Arik shouted and pointed to the other hill.

Near the top of the hill, a dome of light shone, illuminating a group of three people who were struggling to regain their footing after landing. The heat from the light cleared the fog between the hills.

From her side of the valley, Dinah could see the couple were as beautiful as angels. A halo surrounded the male. He looked magnificent, Dinah thought. The woman seemed injured, and she leaned on the man to stand upright. The other man didn't look like an angel, but he had a formidable presence. He looked injured as well and could barely stand by himself.

The light covering the three shimmered and then vanished.

"How did we get here, Arik?" Ciaran's question pulled Dinah's thoughts back to their current situation.

Arik said, "From the creek down the hill outside Mon Ciel, we time traveled to the US in 1864. You seem to have lost track of that period of time, Ciaran. You played a part—"

"What part?"

Madeline cut in. "That's not important now."

"She's right," Arik agreed. "To answer your question, whatever we did back then gave me the ability to trigger my time traveling. I intended to take us back to 2017, at Henley-on-Thames. Because it was the first time I'd done it, I expected it to be bumpy. It was like driving a spaceship of light. It went well until their ball of light appeared out of nowhere and knocked us down here. I don't know where—or when—we are."

"They should get a multiversal driver's license," Dinah said.

"That is, if they were driving," Ciaran said and turned to look again at the trio on the other hill.

The people across the valley looked back, observing.

"Maybe they think we need a driver's license, too. I can't read their minds yet, but I can tell they're not Xiilok creatures. And they're not human, either," Madeline said.

"I think they're friendly," Ciaran said.

"I agree," Dinah said.

"I'm not sure," Arik muttered.

A foggy valley rested between the two hills. The fog was so thick it was impossible to judge how deep the valley was.

Ciaran inched toward the edge of the cliff and peered down. He shook his head, seeing nothing, then turned around. "You can't tell where we are or in what time period, Arik?"

Arik shook his head.

Dinah pointed to her wrist unit. "I can search."

Ciaran said, "Don't, Dinah. My unit works, too. But technology is traceable. Until we know exactly where we are, I don't like the possibility of us being tracked. When Arik time-travels smoothly, it's only the time dimension we have to deal with.

But this time, we were in a collision during travel, and I don't know how far we were pushed out of our original path—or how many dimensions we've crossed."

"No, no, don't use that unit!" Dinah shouted as she saw the formidable man on the other hill about to adjust his wrist unit. Her cries stopped him from proceeding, but he didn't seem to hear what she was saying.

"It's too far away for them to hear us," Arik said.

"That wrist unit is Eudaizian technology. I'm sure of it," Ciaran said.

"The woman over there is thinking *'The dark energy of the demon is coming back, and Sciphil Three won't last long,'*" Madeline said after she peeked randomly into the trio's minds.

"Sciphil Three? Isn't that you?" Dinah asked Ciaran.

"Yes, I am the current king Sciphil. That means the man over there is either Sciphil Three in the past or the future," Ciaran said.

"I can only travel to the past, so he has to be one your ancestors," Arik said.

"Yes, but with the collision on the way here, we have no idea where we are now," Ciaran said.

"Whoever he is, he looks injured. Can you channel to him, Madeline?"

"I've tried. If he's a Sciphil, it should work, but it didn't."

"If you think they're friendly, I can fly over there to have a conversation with them," Dinah said.

"No!" everyone objected at the same time.

Dinah shrugged.

Then they saw a flash in the sky, and another ball of light exploded in mid-air, its remnants tumbling down into the valley. From the wreckage on the fog-covered ground, an old man with long gray hair stepped out. His body expanded, and he grew into a giant humanlike creature nearly fifty feet tall. He turned to look at the trio.

"It looks like he's going to eat those three for brunch!" Arik said.

"Any new information, Madeline?" Ciaran asked.

"The angelic man calls this creature Roallix. He thinks he's not going to be able to protect his wife and Sciphil Three. He's going to make a sacrifice," Madeline said.

"How?" Dinah asked. "Can we help them?"

"All seven of us wouldn't even make a good snack for this hulk. And we don't have a gun. Do you have a strategy, Dinah?" Arik asked.

"Not yet." For the first time, Dinah missed her business partner, Cooper. He would be perfect in this situation. For now, though, Ciaran was their best bet.

Roallix turned toward the trio. He stood as tall as the hill now. For some strange reason, Dinah could sense the action the angelic man from the other hill was going to take. And he did just as she predicted.

He spread his magnificent wings and flew straight at Roallix. Dinah followed suit, spreading her artificial wings and flying at the giant from behind. She pumped her most lethal needles into the back of his head. The behemoth turned around to look at Dinah, simultaneously taking a lightning strike to the head from the angelic man.

Dinah and the man retreated to their respective hillsides.

Roallix looked back and forth between the two hills. He roared but didn't look injured. He certainly wasn't dying from Dinah's needles.

"I think you've merely tickled him with your needles!" Arik said.

Roallix roared again and hunched down, preparing himself to attack.

Ciaran punched a button on his wrist unit, and a dome of translucent white light covered them just before Roallix slammed his shoulder into the hill.

"This is a taste of Eudaizian technology," Ciaran said.

There was a clanking sound, and then Roallix bounced back to the middle of the valley. Not being able to attack this hillside, he turned toward the other.

From that side, Sciphil Three punched a similar button on his wrist unit. A white dome of light covered the trio.

Angry, Roallix slammed a fist onto the white dome. It caved in a bit.

"He's definitely from the past," Ciaran said. "Their protective shield isn't as strong as what we have now."

Seeing the effect he had on the dome, Roallix hit it again and again, the din increasing with every punch. In no time, he would tear a hole right through it.

CHAPTER 18

Arik squinted at the three on the other hill. It was quite a distance, but he could feel the energy coming out of their light dome. Roallix continued to strike the dome, and sooner or later, it would cave in. It would be the end of the trio. He didn't know them, and it was really none of his business if they were killed. Ciaran was protecting the four of them on this hill with his shield. All Arik had to do was to initiate time travel again to bring his group back to Henley-on-Thames, 2017.

Ciaran looked up from his wrist unit. He hadn't previously wanted to use technology, but they had already been exposed, and sooner or later, their adversaries would come regardless.

"Our current setting is 1864, Scotland," Ciaran said.

"Well, this is closer to Henley-on-Thames than the US," Arik muttered.

"I can't yet connect with the unit of the Sciphil Three over there." Ciaran shook his head as he tried to adjust the command on his wrist unit.

"I've got a signal, Ciaran," Madeline said after a long time attempting to psychically connect. "The man over there is Sciphil Three—Malachi LeBlanc."

The hulk Roallix continued his attack on the other dome.

They saw Malachi LeBlanc pull out a Eudaizian gun.

"He can't shoot from inside the dome, so he's going to come out. That's suicidal," Ciaran said and approached the wall of their own dome.

"You can't go out there without a plan, Ciaran," Arik said.

"Well, do you have one, Arik?"

"No, but I'm working on it." Arik paced back and forth. He stared at the angelic man on the other side. *What a magnificent creature*, he thought.

Then he felt a prick on the back of his neck, and a voice said, "My name is Jael. I am the angel of light. What's your name?"

In his mind, Arik replied, "Arik."

"I can tell you're not an angel, so why do you have the light?"

"I don't know. But can I use it to help?"

"Try it. *Will* the light in your mind to hit Roallix."

"I don't know how to do that."

"Concentrate. I can see the light in you. Follow my guidance, and you can use it as a weapon."

Arik followed the instructions Jael channeled into his mind. He gathered the energy of the light Jael said he had inside him, shaped it, and fired.

It didn't move a hair on Roallix's head. Instead, Roallix punched the light dome even harder. It couldn't withstand many more strikes.

"The woman is Charmine," Madeline said after she finished another round of mind spying. "She thinks Roallix wants her, and she wants to come out."

"Surely Malachi and her man won't let her go outside the dome," Dinah said.

They heard a loud bang, and a crack appeared in the dome.

Malachi pulled his king Sciphil sword out.

"I'll need that sword," Ciaran said.

"What are you saying, Ciaran?" Madeline asked.

"That's the king Sciphil sword. It will belong to me in the future. That means I can control it. If I have my sword, I can kill that hulk. My mind blades would kill him, but they'll be too large. I might hit the other dome. But if I get the sword, I can focus my energy into it."

Madeline closed her eyes.

Arik knew she was channeling to Sciphil Three. He took the opportunity to re-connect with Jael. Jael looked over and nodded.

"Ciaran, if I get you to the middle of the valley, and you can get the sword, are you sure you can kill the hulk, or will you just become its next meal?" Arik asked.

"If you can get me the sword, I'll take care of the rest," Ciaran said.

Arik nodded at Jael. The angel turned to say something to Malachi. Jael nodded to Arik and channeled a plan into his mind.

The large crack made its way from the top of the dome downward. One more strike, and it would all be over.

"Are you ready, Ciaran?" Arik asked.

"Yes."

"Open our dome," Arik said.

Ciaran opened the dome immediately. From the other hillside, Sciphil Three from the past opened theirs.

Roallix stopped in confusion. Before he could react, Jael opened his palms. His eyes went blank, and from his palms, a light bridge appeared, arching over the valley.

Arik opened his palms exactly the same way Jael did. He had received Jael's instructions to summon the light force, but now he could feel Jael holding his hands, guiding him to draw and control the energy. He did exactly as Jael did.

The two light beams from Jael connected immediately to Arik's hands, drawing the light out from Arik. Together, they formed a bridge of sparkling light from one hilltop to the other.

Asking no questions, Ciaran charged to the bridge. "Give me the sword!" he shouted as he ran over it.

From the other side, Sciphil Three darted toward the bridge and jumped onto it.

The light bridge was incredible, but Arik could not be sure it was solid or strong enough for the two kings of Eudaiz, one from the past and one from the future, to run on. Did they trust him and the angel on the other hillside, or was it just an innate ability leaders had to know when they must rely on the resources of others to accomplish a mission?

Madeline channeled to Charmine, "The hulk is going to break the light bridge."

Charmine turned her head in Madeline's direction and nodded to acknowledge she had received the signal. She sat down on the grass and closed her eyes. She began to chant.

Roallix had turned toward the bridge and was about to hurl his body at it.

Ciaran and Sciphil Three still ran toward the middle of the bridge.

Then the giant just stopped, frozen as if it couldn't move. It roared in anger.

Jael glanced quickly at Charmine and then returned to holding the light bridge still.

From her side, Madeline could see Charmine's eyes go blank. She said to Dinah, "She's chanting some sort of song from the traveler's spirit. It's holding the hulk immobile. It's not a curse. She seems to be using her old energy. I don't think she's going to last long. Could you fly out there just in case the two men on the bridge fall?"

"Sure." Dinah spread her wings and flew into the air.

Ciaran and Malachi met at the halfway point on the light bridge. Malachi thrust his sword to Ciaran.

Unable to move, Roallix roared in anger, exhaling a stream of fire toward the bridge. Malachi fell over the edge. Dinah swooped under the bridge to catch him.

Ciaran grabbed the sword. He concentrated and gathered his mind blade energy. By itself, his mind blade could dig up the entire hill. But that wasn't what he wanted. He needed to focus and send all his power into the sword.

He glanced quickly toward the other hill. He didn't know what Charmine was doing, but he understood she was somehow holding the hulk still for him.

He knew he had only one shot.

In a single swift move, he swung the sword, injected with his energy. The force coming off the sword was a mighty blade glowing with energy and fire.

Roallix's head was chopped off. His body crumbled and disintegrated, exploding into nothingness.

The force of the strike threw Ciaran backward. He fell off the bridge. Dinah was waiting beneath it, and she grabbed him with her free hand. Then she flapped her wings and flew toward the far hill.

"I never imagined two king Sciphils would be so heavy!" she yelled down to them as she descended quickly toward the hilltop. Once she was about ten feet from the ground, she dropped the men, and they rolled on the grass.

"Thank you," Ciaran said, standing up. He helped Malachi stand as well. "Are you okay?" he asked.

"Yes, and you?"

Ciaran nodded.

Jael withdrew the light bridge and turned around. "My wife," he rushed over to Charmine, who had collapsed on the ground from exhaustion.

After a quick circle in the air to reduce her momentum, Dinah landed. She hurried over to Charmine. "Let me see if I can help."

Ciaran also approached Charmine to take her pulse.

From the ground, she looked up, smiling at Jael. "Don't worry, I'm just tired," she said.

"The injury to your leg is severe," Dinah said. As soon as she touched Charmine, her body flew into the air like a rag doll and smashed into a rock outcropping nearby. She slid lifelessly down to the bottom of the rock and passed out on the ground.

Ciaran ran to Dinah, and Jael grabbed Charmine.

From the other hill, Madeline was letting Arik know what was happening.

Arik summoned all his power and shot the light bridge over the valley without Jael's help. Ciaran picked up Dinah and charged to the other side of the bridge.

From the other side, Sciphil Three of the past opened the portal. Before they telecasted away, Jael's voice echoed back, "We will be seeing each other again."

Then they vanished.

Ciaran leaped to the ground with Dinah, and Arik withdrew the bridge. His excessive use of power had taken a lot of energy out of him. He slumped to the ground and spat out some blood.

After Madeline helped Arik up, he said, "Let's go!" He grabbed Madeline's hand then ran over to grab Ciaran's shoulder as he carried Dinah in his arms.

They traveled back. This time, there was no collision.

PART TWO

CHAPTER 19

The muddy black substance mixed with his basic elements and his soul to form his new flesh and blood. Roallix's mind floated around, observing his own reformation. *Do I have a soul at all?* he thought. Then he let the thought go as it was no longer relevant to his situation.

He had made several mistakes over the hundreds of years of his lifespan across the multiverse. But this one was the worst. He should have trusted his partners in crime. No, he should have let them do their part.

The reformation was excruciatingly slow. Mostly because the hit he had copped on Earth had destroyed his body. He was lucky he had chosen the magical world as his foundation and had never crossed worlds. Otherwise, the reformation wouldn't have been possible.

What the heck just happened?

He knew he shouldn't have attacked Jael and Charmine. It was too rushed. But he thought with the giant form he had taken he could crush them with his fists. When they had a collision in the middle of the multiversal transitional zone, Roallix saw opportunity falling into his lap. It was blind luck that he'd defeated Jael a long time ago. He couldn't be blamed for taking a chance when it came his way.

He had underestimated the humanlike creatures who had collided with Charmine and Jael. It was none of their business that he had attacked Jael and Charmine. *Why had they interfered?* That was a hell of a weapon they had used on him.

"You know I can destroy you right now, and you will never be able to reform, Roallix."

Normally he would have turned around to see the incoming guest, but his body was only half-formed, so instead, he turned his mind's eye and saw Asana.

"You promised me you'd break them!" Roallix growled. He'd intended a roar but was too weak at the moment.

"We shouldn't have let you take the magical world circle with your feeble mind. You aren't built to be an angel. If I made a creature of mud, it would be smarter than you are."

"Don't insult me!" he coughed.

"I rest my case." Asana shook his head then sighed. "We have invested much in you, and so I'll give you one last chance to reform and take your part."

"If I had learned nothing in my centuries' long association with you, I would believe you. But I know you too well. You can't afford to replace me now. It takes three of us to make the circles. Arete is recuperating after being hit by a random citizen of the multiverse. If you destroy me, the plan you've built over hundreds of years will suffer. And you don't have another five hundred years to wait."

Asana nodded. "I see you're not stupid. But for your information, Arete wasn't hit by a *random* citizen of the multiverse. It was Cooper Donovan from Iilos. And I examined Arete's wounds. They were caused by Eudaizian technology."

"And?"

Asana shifted his stance in agitation. "Maybe you're not stupid, but you're arrogant and ignorant, Roallix. Eudaiz is our biggest challenge in both the material world and the Amalgam world. And Iilos, the sub-dimensional universe that Cooper comes from, is a strong ally of Eudaiz."

"Let me ask again, Asana, why is this relevant to me? I take care of the magical world. You deal with the Amalgam, and Arete is supposed to handle the material world. It will work only if you each complete your part! If the deal isn't going well, I'll be very happy to take my magical world. I don't need you. I don't care what you have to deal with. I don't need the full circles. So *don't* tell me what to do!"

Asana nodded. "All right then. I thought I'd offer a potion that would lock in your reformation. But it seems you don't need me." He turned and walked away, muttering, "Next time you get hit by a Eudaizian weapon, you won't be so lucky."

"I can hear you," Roallix said.

Asana turned around. "It's too late. I've decided Arete and I don't need you anymore. We'll find another partner to take the magical world circle."

"There isn't anyone who can replace me!"

Asana laughed. "As a matter of fact, I have someone in mind that may be even more qualified than you. He's expensive, but he's worth every bit of the investment. Plus, he doesn't have any baggage."

"If you had someone, you would have traded me in a long time ago. Don't bluff. It doesn't suit you."

Asana smirked and shrugged. Then he walked away and vanished into another dimension.

Anger consumed Roallix so badly that smoke rolled out of his reforming body. If he had a body, he could crush a mountain with his bare hands.

He had never paid attention to worlds other than his own magical one. He belonged to the magical world and had worked and sacrificed for it. He deserved everything magic had to offer him. That focus had kept him in this world for years without crossing.

He had never thought the material world, including the multiverse and the universes within it, could be so powerful. He had let that world go for a long time. It had always been tempting for him. There, he could find all the things he had once had when he was human—money, power, sex. And those things comprised only a fraction of what the material world could offer.

Asana said Roallix had been struck by a Eudaizian weapon. He knew of Eudaiz. If those creatures on the hills had been Eudaizians, then perhaps he should give this matter some attention.

You mortal sons of bitches, he cursed in his mind, thinking of the creature swinging a sword at him and destroying his body.

Roallix's mind smiled at his almost formed body, and he could see a face with lips forming a smile. It wasn't yet perfect, though, and might scare children in the material world.

But he knew magic—and with that, he could do almost anything to all creatures in the material world and the Amalgam world combined.

Regardless of how powerful they were, they were mortal.

CHAPTER 20

Cooper whirled back and forth between two giant pieces of icy rock the size of football stadiums.

"Where the hell are we?" he asked himself.

"I thought you said we were going back to Iilos for safety," Jenny said.

He didn't realize he had spoken his thoughts out loud. "That was the plan. But as I've mentioned, we didn't exactly use a good teleporting channel, so we were dumped in the middle of nowhere."

Jenny glanced around. "Can you contact someone?" she asked.

He could tell she was nervous, and he was responsible for that. She'd trusted him.

The place looked like a desert, with its endless red dirt hills and strange looking giant cacti. But the elusive environment around them was what scared Jenny and made her nervous.

The two large rocks they had just seen had morphed into a dark lake. The water was so black Cooper could imagine creatures from the cosmos jumping out from the depths to attack them. An ever-changing environment like this could only come from two places he knew of—the Daimon Gate or Xiilok.

If they had ended up in the Daimon Gate, it would be their lucky day. The Daimon Gate was like the Interpol of the multiverse. Only criminals and unworthy creatures had to worry about the Daimon Gate. But if this was Xiilok, they were in very deep trouble.

Cooper promised himself if he ever got out of this situation, he'd never ever use the cheap multiversal public teleport system again. He wanted to turn on the wrist unit Ciaran had given him but was afraid using the technology would enable his adversaries to trace him.

"Jenny, I won't contact anyone just yet, not until I find out exactly where we are. Using technology will reveal our location to others. And there are a lot of badasses in the multiverse."

"Understood." She smiled.

He wanted to kiss those lips right now. Jenny didn't have an explosive and sexually appealing figure like his sexual partners in Iilos. He realized just now he had not thought of them as girlfriends. Even in Iilos, the term girlfriend had sentimental value. He had been casual about relationships before. But something in him had changed. He wasn't sure it was for the good, but he knew he wanted to protect Jenny.

"If we run into some shady characters, I can fight them, you know." Jenny winked at him.

"But you practice aikido, right? Isn't that for self-defense and not attack?"

"What I meant is, I can defend myself, and I can protect you—when it's convenient." She grinned.

"Yes, ma'am. But I've got this." He pulled out his restraint bands. "I kept these from the days I worked as a bounty hunter. If I tie them on a creature, no power in the multiverse can free it.

How about you let me take care of the situation, okay? Until we can take you back home safe and sound."

The shadow of a creature appeared in the thick fog, walking toward them.

Cooper pushed Jenny behind him.

"Can you please not push me behind you? I can take care of myself."

"I'm sure you can. But I'm the one who got you here, and it's my responsibility to keep you safe. You've never dealt with creatures in the multiverse."

The creature came closer. It appeared to be a harmless old man, carrying a basket in his hand. His eyes were focused on the ground, and he was stooped over to pick up something Cooper and Jenny couldn't see.

Looking up and seeing them, the man startled and stepped backward, bumping his back against the rock behind him.

Cooper raised a hand to calm the old man down. "We don't mean any harm. Do you speak English?"

Iilos, Cooper's native language, was English with an Irish accent, for reasons he didn't understand. But he hoped Jenny could naturally pick up what the man said if he did speak English. He also wanted to withhold his true identity.

The man looked at them and said in Xiilok, "You from Earth?"

Cooper's Xiilok wasn't good, but he could communicate well enough. He translated back to Jenny and then responded, "Yes."

The man chuckled. "We must really be heading toward doomsday. Even humans can make it to the multiverse now." He shook his head in despair.

"What do you mean?" Cooper asked.

"Creatures from different worlds mixing together will contaminate all the worlds."

"You speak Xiilok, but you don't have the usual wormy eyes. Are you a mix yourself?"

The man raised an eyebrow. "You're knowledgeable, young human."

"So is this Xiilok?"

"No. It's the transitional zone bordering Xiilok. If you enter Xiilok, don't drink the water at the gate. It'll give you wormy eyes." The man smiled and nodded a goodbye. Then he turned and focused on picking wildflowers from the ground.

Cooper shook his head. He hadn't seen the flowers on the ground before. He turned around, wrapped his arm around Jenny's waist, and steered her away, whispering, "Let him go away. I'll use my unit to navigate our way out of here. The Xiilok border is dangerous, and when I use my unit, we'll have targets on our backs."

Jenny nodded and maintained a neutral expression.

From a short distance away, they heard a low growl in the thick fog. A space wolf creature crept out and charged at the old man. He held up his flower basket in an effort to block the attack, but the wolf was too strong. It pushed him to the ground and landed on him, its gigantic front paws on the man's chest.

Its teeth were bared, and it was about to rip the man's throat out.

"No, Jenny!" Cooper shouted, but it was too late. Jenny had charged past him toward the wolf. She grabbed at its back and tail, sidestepped to gain momentum, and then in one swift swing, she yanked the wolf off the man.

Cooper rushed over to pull Jenny away. The man scrambled up from the ground. He picked up his flower basket and threw it at Cooper. The flowers poured out from the basket and rained down on him.

Cooper inhaled the dust and powder from the flowers. Before he knew what was happening, his throat started to close, his world became blurry, and his knees buckled.

"Cooper!"

He felt Jenny's arms wrapping around his shoulders.

"Cooper, don't scare me."

He gasped for air. The old man approached and crouched.

"Get away from him!" Jenny pulled Cooper backward. "What do you want?"

The man reached out and, fast as lightning, grabbed Cooper's right arm and pressed. Jenny kicked the man away. On Cooper's wrist, his Iilos wrist unit emerged. He was a native Iilos citizen. Thus the wrist unit—his personal identification—was embedded into his body.

"You're Cooper Donovan. The only Iilos wandering this no-man's-land." The man chuckled.

Cooper lay on the ground. He had seen Jenny charge at the man and had thought he had been totally wrong to think she wouldn't attack just because she studied aikido.

"What did you do? You fix him, or I'll break your neck!"

Cooper thought he'd believe her if he were that man. The man turned and grew nearly ten feet tall. But Jenny didn't hesitate. She used momentum to supplement her disadvantage in size and strength. She attacked him with a torrent of punches, kicks, pushes, and twists, all that her human body could possibly give out.

Cooper could see the man was intrigued by her tenacity. He could kill her with a flick of his finger, but he played around and let her fight.

Behind Jenny, the wolf had now shifted into a tall creature that walked on two legs but still had a wolf's head. It grabbed her from behind. It was bigger than she was and lifted her off the ground.

The man approached Cooper and crouched. "You don't know as much as you think you do. Native Iilos should never go near wolfsbane. Not the flower, but the chemical I compounded. Now I've told you I'll have to kill you. But not before I use your wrist unit."

He raised a finger to stop Cooper before he could respond.

"I know the unit works only when you're alive, and it will work only with your command. I have no intention of extracting its technology over your dead body, so don't worry, I'll keep you alive."

Then he looked at the wolf creature and said, "Get rid of her."

"I have the secret inside Mon Ciel," Cooper said.

"Stop!" the man called out to the wolf creature.

"Asana, are you sure?" the creature asked.

"Are you questioning me?"

It shook its head.

"I want to talk to Jenny," Cooper said.

Asana smirked. "I'll see what I can do." He looked at the creature. "Let her go."

It released Jenny. As soon as her feet hit the ground, she rushed toward Cooper. He reached his hand up, and she grabbed it. "Please don't die, Cooper."

He hated to see tears rolling down that pretty face. "I'd run for my life as soon as my feet hit the ground if I were you."

"Then who's going to save you?"

He pulled out a restraint band in his pocket and snapped her hand to his hand. He looked at Asana and said, "If she loses a hair, you've got nothing." Then he passed out.

CHAPTER 21

Arik hung up the phone and looked at Ciaran and Madeline. They were back in their current time, and Ciaran had placed them in an exclusive high-rise apartment in the middle of vibrant London.

Ciaran's philosophy was that the most secure place would be right under the enemy's nose, where it appeared to be the least secure. Although Ciaran had blocked out the top five floors for exclusivity, Arik's stomach still churned whenever he saw the shadow of anyone walking in the foyer or out on the street.

Arik admired Ciaran for his leadership ability. He'd never told Ciaran that and made a mental note to himself that he must learn some of Ciaran's skills to use when he became the leader of the Yellow Shield tribe in Xiilok. He was too jumpy to think about that now. He had almost punched the security officer at the car park when his phone went off suddenly with a *Star Wars* sword-swinging jingle. Ciaran had had to pull him away and threaten to drug him to calm him down.

"So?" Ciaran asked, leaning back in the three-seater sofa located at the center of the endless marble-floored living room.

"Jenny and Cooper are definitely not in New York with Mother."

"But my signals locate them there," Ciaran said.

"You tagged my sister?"

"No, I tagged Cooper. That's how I find out where my people are and keep them safe." He turned toward Madeline. "Have you sensed anything, Madeline?"

She shook her head.

"Oh, hey you, what are you doing out here?" Arik asked as Dinah walked into the living room. The shiny surface of the marble floor reflected the light onto her porcelain skin, making her look even more frail.

"I'm not an invalid."

"No, Dinah Greenwoods is not. But a person with severe head injury, a broken shoulder, a broken arm, a broken leg, and three cracked ribs would be!"

"I heal quicker than humans."

"Oh, I forgot, you're not human. But I have more important things to worry about now. Like my human sister, my human mother, and my human father." Arik gestured in frustration.

Ciaran stepped quickly toward Dinah and took her to the sofa. He took her vitals at her wrist on the way. "You're recovering much faster than I expected," Ciaran said and smiled.

"He always thinks Eudaizians with Silver Blood are the best," Madeline said and grinned. "Welcome back, Dinah."

"I don't die that easily." She jiggled the button on the shoulder of her jacket. "I'm glad the fall didn't break my wings."

"If the weapon is broken, I can always make you another. But I can't fix you if you are broken. It was blind luck this time. Have you been able to figure out why you flew backward into the rock?" Ciaran asked.

"Not yet. And it's not a priority right now. Have you found Cooper and Jenny?"

Ciaran shook his head and turned toward Arik. "You've never mentioned your father before. Why now?"

Arik shrugged. "I don't know. Mother asked me three times what's up with Jenny. I had to lie to her to stop her from worrying. Then she asked what's up with my dad and me." He started to pace the floor. "I haven't spoken to him for more than a year. She said he called asking to meet with her and asked her not to tell me. He's never done that before."

"Never done what? Call your mother, or ask her not to tell you about the meeting?" Dinah asked.

"He doesn't use a telephone."

"He's anti-technology?" Madeline asked.

Ciaran shook his head. "I don't think so. Diana told me he managed the electrical production department at a theater before they moved to New York. His job was high-tech. He can't have been anti-technology and specialize in communication devices in that industry."

Arik nodded. "Yes, Mother said he used to be technologically savvy. Then something happened, and he freaked out even with low-tech equipment like radios..." Arik trailed off, turned around, and looked at everyone.

"Do you think he had anything to do with this?" Dinah asked.

Ciaran, booting up a small computer, said nothing. Dinah opened her mouth to speak, but Ciaran raised a finger to stop her. "I've isolated the network," he said. "There's no signal coming out from this one."

"Dinah, knowing Cooper, do you think he would have given Diana something to bring back to New York, something Ciaran might have a tracking device embedded in? A gift of some sort?" Madeline asked.

Dinah shook her head. "I'm not sure. He's a very good guy. But he's not the sentimental type. At least, until Jenny—"

"Excuse me!" Arik exclaimed.

"Hello, I have eyes," Dinah said. "Native Iilos don't show much sentiment. But when they meet the right mate, it shows. He was drooling when he met Jenny. I think he's falling for her."

"That's sexual attraction, not sentiment, Dinah," Arik said.

"Okay, let's just focus. I just want to know why Ciaran's tracking devices on Cooper ended up in New York when he and Jenny clearly aren't there," Madeline said.

"Oh, I think I know," Dinah said. "My jacket was torn off when Arik and I got stuck in the tree, and Cooper showed up with Diana's jacket. He said they heard the sound of fabric being torn via the speaker phone, and Diana thought I might need some cover."

"That's right," Arik said. "Then you didn't need Mother's jacket because you were wearing mine. I think Cooper held on to that jacket. He might have left something in it before giving it back to Mother."

"A pen," Ciaran said while still working on his computer.

"You tracked his pen?" Arik asked.

"Yes, and that's what is giving me the signal now."

"Why don't you give your mother a call and ask her if she can find Cooper's pen in her jacket?" Madeline asked.

"If I call her one more time about Cooper and Jenny, she will definitely freak out." He dialed the phone.

Ciaran looked up from his computer. "I found something on your father. Before moving to New York, he was in an explosion in the Tri-Sun Group headquarters. Tri-Sun is, or was, one of the most notorious high-tech groups. They dissolved after that incident."

"What do you know about them?" Dinah asked. "Do you want me to run a search, Ciaran?"

"They're into solar energy, and they might have nothing at all to do with our current situation..." Ciaran said. "I've got a signal. It's from Cooper's cell."

Ciaran's fingers flew over the keyboard as he analyzed the data.

Then he looked up. "The cell I gave him was activated in Xiilok, not by him, but by Jenny. And that's an alarm signal." He slammed the computer shut and stood up.

On the phone Arik was using to call his mother, there was a sound of someone answering, and his father's voice said,

"Arik?"

Then the sound of an explosion echoed out of the speaker, and the line went dead.

CHAPTER 22

Malachi stopped the teleport at the transitional zone of the multiverse. It was close to Eudaiz, and it was much safer for him to take Charmine and Jael there. But it would mean crossing the dead zone for Charmine. He had taken her there once without knowing her condition. He would never do that again.

He was king of Eudaiz, and with his power, he could do a lot. But there was nothing he could do about the natural conditions of his universe, like the way Eudaizians gave birth.

He was really weak at the moment because of Asana's poison. Jael's light could hold him now, but not for much longer. He could only hope they didn't have to engage in another fight.

"You could go closer to Eudaiz," Jael said.

Malachi shook his head. "Charmine couldn't handle another pass."

"But you said we could bring you back to Eudaiz if we wore the bracelets."

"I wasn't all together when I said that. I meant you could bring me to the border. The bracelets secure your and Charmine's profiles. You can pass to any dimension whenever you want without your profiles changing. But the bracelets can't secure your child."

Charmine stirred in Jael's arms and opened her eyes. She smiled at him. "Put me down, will you?"

Jael put her down and leaned her gently against a large rock.

"Do you remember what just happened? What you did to the giant hulk and how you shot that girl to the rock?" Malachi asked her.

Jael's eyes darkened. He said nothing and turned away.

Charmine smiled at him, but Malachi could see the sadness in her eyes. What she did must have been a major decision.

"I didn't hurt the girl. I don't know why that happened. To immobilize the giant creature, I summoned the spirit of the traveler's God—the God of free spirit. And in doing so, I owe him a favor that he might be calling for in the future."

Malachi shook his head. "So the God immobilized the creature for you because you prayed to him. If you are his subject, then he should do what you pray for without holding you to a debt."

She smiled. "You accept the fact that I am a gypsy of the multiverse. You also must accept the idea of a free spirit. We are free to travel, free to stay. We do everything according to our own will, until we go against nature. The giant creature was free to move according to its will until I forced it to stop. As a result, it was killed. I went against nature and the free spirit of my tribe."

"You did that in defense, to protect us," Malachi said.

"Yes, but the creature had nothing to do with the God I prayed to. The God didn't have to immobilize it and get it killed. He acted against the creature's free will because of me. So the fault was on me. That's our tribe's religion."

"But you left that tribe a long time ago. You don't belong with them," Jael growled.

"Jael, don't be angry. Once a gypsy, always a gypsy. I am proud of my origins."

"I don't condemn you for it. But it put you in danger."

"I'm not worried. I have your protection. I am your subject, and you are a good angel."

"My protection? See what it got you?" Jael whirled back and forth in frustration.

Malachi looked into Charmine's deep hazel eyes and could see she was fading quickly. "Jael," he called out.

"What?" Jael turned around and saw what Malachi was seeing. He rushed over. "Charmine, please don't go. Please tell me what to do."

She gripped the grass, and sweat streamed down her forehead. In front of them, her tummy swelled. "I think our child is coming." Her stomach grew from nothingness to a size that looked as if she would give birth any second.

"Tell me what to do, Charmine," Jael cried out.

"I'll go get the medical doctor in Eudaiz," Malachi said, but he knew it was too late. The travel, the collision, the magic fight, and too many crossings had taken a toll on her. But he couldn't explain why the baby was coming now.

Charmine dug her fingers into the grass and soil and said nothing. She breathed heavily, looking as if she would fade away shortly.

"Malachi, do something," Jael said.

"I can't scientifically explain this. You're an angel, and *you* don't know what to do. How do you expect *me* to fix this? We'd better hope for a miracle!"

From behind them, they heard footsteps and chanting, the clattering and clanking of metal and bells in the wind.

From the fog emerged spears, horned heads, hooded heads, and then groups of humanlike creatures in long cloaks. Malachi drew his sword. Jael glowed and tightened his fists, a sign that he was ready to strike with his light.

"No, that's my tribe," Charmine said weakly, her eyes closed.

She knew they would come for her, Malachi thought. As far as he was concerned, this was the miracle they were looking for, their only way out of this situation.

An old man with long white hair, wearing a brown and gold cloak, approached. "I am the shaman. I delivered Charmine into our world. Now I can help her child."

"Our child has been cursed," Charmine said.

The shaman inched forward. Jael stopped him. "Don't you dare touch her!"

"She's in pain, and they can help," Malachi said.

"How do you know?"

"I don't know for sure. But we have no other options. If she doesn't get help, she'll die."

"Let him help me, please, Jael. I don't care if I die. But I want our child to be born before I do," Charmine cried out.

Jael whirled around. "You're not going to die!"

"Then let her get help. There's nothing you can do now." Malachi pulled Jael aside. He knew Jael could toss him like a rag doll with his power, and in his deteriorating condition, he would likely crack his skull and die. But he could see that Jael wasn't thinking straight at the moment, so he continued to move him away from the shaman.

Jael calmed down quickly. He turned and spoke to the shaman. "I apologize. Please help my wife."

The shaman nodded and approached Charmine.

Jael followed.

The shaman stopped. "This is a sacred ritual. You cannot watch."

"But I am the father of the child."

The shaman stood still and wouldn't move.

Malachi pulled at Jael's elbow. "Come on, let's just go around to the other side of the rock."

Jael reluctantly followed Malachi. It was only a short while they waited, but it seemed like centuries. Eventually, a child's cry brightened Jael's face. He rushed around the rock, over to where Charmine had been.

But there was no sign of his wife or the tribe, only the emptiness of the air.

The child's cry still echoed in the air, hovering, and then it faded out.

Jael whirled around. Malachi was speechless.

"Charmine!" Jael roared. But all he heard now was the echo of his own voice.

CHAPTER 23

Jenny tiptoed over to a tiny window and peeked outside, but she couldn't see much. She wasn't short, but the window was tailored for a ten-foot-tall man—if you could call someone that size that a man. She didn't understand the language the old man had used to talk with Cooper, but she was sure Cooper was trying to make a deal for her safety before he passed out.

The creature in the shape of an old man had left the room. He hadn't bothered tying them up. He hadn't even secured the door, confident that an unconscious Cooper would be a living shackle.

He might be right.

She looked at Cooper closely. He was beautiful. Striking blue eyes, a masculine face, and a killer smile. She didn't know his hometown or his life in a universe she had never visited. But judging by the way he maintained his friendship with Dinah, he was a trustworthy person—or creature.

She smiled to herself and wondered if Iilos citizens referred to themselves as people or entities. They certainly wouldn't call themselves alien in their own universe.

Cooper stirred and groggily opened his eyes.

"Hey!" She brushed the stray hair from his forehead. "You're alive!"

He smiled, too tired to say anything. She didn't know what kind of powder the old man had used on Cooper, but it had had no effect on her at all, except for the lingering bad odor.

"Before you dump tons of your theory on me about what happened, just know that whatever deal you made with that old man—and I'm not sure if he's really a man—he left us alone, literally."

Cooper glanced around. She helped him sit up. She twisted her arm around, trying to find a comfortable position. Cooper jiggled the restraint band that tied their hands together and flipped out a small tag. He was about to enter a code.

"Wait, the man left us without securing us. He's obviously relying on the fact that you can't free yourself. Maybe he didn't expect you'd wake. Or maybe he put something in this band so that it'll explode if you open it."

Cooper laughed, but it turned into a fit of wheezing and coughing due to his weakness. She patted his back gently. "Take it easy. Do you know what he did to you?"

He shook his head. She looked into his eyes, and she knew he was lying.

"We need to get out of here. He probably thinks I won't wake soon, and that's why he didn't lock the place up."

"All right." She helped him up. He entered the code and yanked the band open to free their hands.

"When I say run, you have to run really fast, all right?" he said.

"Okay."

"I'm serious."

"Yes, Cooper. Let's get out of here."

Before they left the house, Cooper slid a small device under the seat of a stone bench.

"I switched your cell on and sent distress signals already," said Jenny.

"You did what?"

"I sent Ciaran an alarm signal from your cell. I saw him give you that phone. I figured the signal would go to him."

Seeing an expression of awe on his face, Jenny explained, "I have an IT degree from MIT, a university where I got quite a sophisticated education. I'm not sure if there's a network here, but I think their technology most likely has some kind of internal mechanism that doesn't rely on a network."

Cooper nodded. "All right, so we've established that technology isn't a problem for you. But one thing you have to remember—in Xiilok, you don't shoot a gun."

"Why not?"

"It's complicated. Just know that you won't ever hit the target. But this will." He pulled out a folded knife from a small pocket in his pants.

"A bottle opener?"

"No, it's a knife, soaked in Dinah's special treatment. She made this for me in case of emergency. She said it's lethal. I'm quite sure it destroys more than bottles." He gave the knife to Jenny.

"I don't need a weapon."

He nodded and slid the knife back into his pocket. "Let's go then."

The world outside the house was unnerving. Jenny had seen many horror movies, including many her college boyfriends couldn't handle, but in front of her now was reality. It was a scene that made those horror movies seem no more than children's cartoons.

Black soil covered the rolling hills. Its uneven surface was covered in shards of strange rocks, craters in the ground, and bare trees that appeared out of nowhere and shifted position as they pleased.

Cooper said, "This is Xiilok. This place is full of dimensional traps. The most important thing to remember is that you'll see what your mind wants to see. What you see doesn't reflect reality. There is no reality in Xiilok. You have to be really careful where you step. We don't want to drop into an oblivion trap."

He turned on his cell phone, and a glowing blue screen appeared.

"There's a cell phone network here?" Jenny asked in astonishment.

"No, this is Eudaizian technology, not just a cell phone. Without this navigator, we have no chance of getting out of here alive. That's why I didn't want you to go when I was out." He showed her the screen. "This is the true map of the landscape. It scans the surface we're walking on and gives possible directions to where we want to go. Remember, we can't rely on our visual sense here because everything is illusional." He thrust the phone into Jenny's hand.

"You're as white as a sheet, Cooper. You want to sit down?"

"No, no time. Keep moving." He walked ahead. "Are we going straight ahead, Jenny? What does the map's indicator show?"

"No, you have to sit down."

"Jenny, we don't have time. You need to learn how to read the map. We're trying to get as close to the transitional zone as possible. From there, navigate to the Daimon Gate. It's the multiversal neutral ground, kind of like the police on Earth."

"Your nose is bleeding, Cooper."

He wiped the blood off and reached for the cell. "It's close enough. Keep walking, Jenny."

"You have to tell me what's going on, or I'm going nowhere."

"Asana put wolfsbane in me, Jenny. It's a poison targeting native Iilos. It corrupts my blood. There's nothing I can do about it."

"There is always a solution. Ciaran will know what to do. I'll send another signal." She grabbed for the phone.

"It will be too late, Jenny. Asana was so sure that I wouldn't dare move to buy time for an antidote. But there is no antidote for this, Jenny. We've just run the distance. The poison has already circulated throughout my blood."

"This is unfair. You can't do this to me."

"We're so close. Look!" He pointed at something that looked like a well. "I've heard about that well. It marks the entrance of Xiilok, and it borders the Daimon Gate."

"All wells look the same, Cooper."

"That's the well of second chances. Drink the water, and you'll turn into a Xiilok creature." Then he swayed and dropped the phone.

Jenny picked it up, supporting him at the same time. She glanced at the map. "The Daimon Gate, is it?" The indicator showed they were actually only about fifty feet from the border. But when she looked up from the screen, she saw nothing.

She clenched her teeth and supported Cooper, dragging the two of them in the general direction that the map said was the border of the Daimon Gate.

Asana stepped out of the fog. He smirked and said, "I'm disappointed you left without saying goodbye!"

CHAPTER 34

Dinah scanned the navigating device across the ground. It took a bit of time to gather sufficient information. She glanced at Arik. He paced back and forth. She knew he was anxious. He had agreed with Ciaran that they should split up their team. Ciaran's had many resources on Earth, so he and Madeline had gone to New York to help Arik's parents. Dinah and Arik had gone to Xiilok to find Jenny and Cooper because of Arik's connection with the Yellow Shield tribe.

Neither Arik nor Ciaran were comfortable with the solution, but they didn't have any other options. One thing they hadn't considered was that Dinah had not only been to Xiilok, she had also lived there until she was five.

She thought she knew the land.

She was wrong.

The little stretch of land she knew as Xiilok was in no way comparable to this side of that universe—what Ciaran referred to as the land of the multiversal outlaws. She couldn't imagine they were talking about the same universe. She knew about this side of Xiilok but had never set foot here—not even on a job.

Arik broke the silence. "Why don't you have wormy eyes?"

"What?" She looked up from the scanner.

"Before we left, Ciaran said Xiilok creatures have wormy eyes. You said you lived here until you were five. Why don't you have wormy eyes?"

"First, I'm not a creature. I was a citizen, and I lived in a residential area. Only those who gain admission through the second chance gate and drink the water at the well have wormy eyes."

"Second chance—it almost sounds noble," Arik said and rolled his eyes.

Dinah chuckled. "Tell me about it. They're mostly shady characters. But as I said, my experience living here is very limited."

"So where did you live before migrating to Iilos?"

"Many places. I was between jobs all the time."

"Between jobs? How old were you when you started working?"

"Arik, never ask a female creature in the multiverse how old she is. She wouldn't know. Even on Earth, you have different time zones. In the multiverse, we have many different time dimensions and time references."

Arik nodded. "Have you found anything yet?"

She shook her head.

"So all citizens here have to use a scanning device for direction? I didn't see any such technology when I was with the Yellow Shield."

"No, it's only on this side that we see nothing." She looked up and glanced around. A continually changing landscape surrounded her.

The tracker suggested they were very close to where Jenny and Cooper were. But in front of them was nothingness. Not even a large rock. And she was sure this wasn't where the Yellow Shield tribe lived. They would be located somewhere in the stretch of land where she used to live.

She glanced at the device. It detected nothing. Why had the device landed them here when she'd asked it to navigate to the Yellow Shield tribe?

"Look out!" Arik shouted and pushed her out of the way of a giant ball of dirt rolling down toward them from what seemed like mid-air.

And then a flash of light exploded on them like a bomb.

***

A cool hand brushing over her face woke Dinah. She opened her eyes and saw a face she didn't ever want to see—possibly for eternity. It was Grace, Arik's drop-dead-gorgeous ex-girlfriend. While she wasn't quite sure about the ex-girlfriend part, she did know for sure she had shattered Grace's pretty head with a laser gun.

Even though she knew she had only shot a space creature disguised as Grace, the idea she had put a beam to the head of a human had never set well with her.

Grace smiled.

Dinah frowned, unsure how to react. *Is this the real Grace or another creature in disguise?*

"You have a lot of injuries. What did you do to yourself?"

Dinah cleared her throat. "Thank you for taking care of me. You don't know me, and there's no way you would know about my injuries unless you scanned my body. But I didn't consent to a scan."

Grace arched an eyebrow and said nothing.

"Did I speak too quickly?"

"I beg your pardon?"

"I like your jacket. Where did you get it?"

Silence.

"Those shoes are killer. I bet you got them in London."

Silence.

Dinah knew then she was speaking to a robot. It wasn't programmed to answer random questions and didn't know how to react to arbitrary statements. She sat up and glanced around the small room, decorated with furniture of stone and wood. The decoration looked ancient, and there was no sign of technology. She didn't seem to be imprisoned.

She saw a flickering candle with real fire. *Not even powered light! Where is this place?*

The door of the room slid open, and Arik walked in with a man who held a flaming torch. Dinah had never seen a torch like that before, but she'd heard of them. She frowned at Arik. He approached and crouched in front of her bed.

"How are you feeling? Look at the bruise on your forehead. I told you you're not fit to take a trip, even if it is a vacation." He gestured around them. "And you can see the outer ring of Xiilok isn't exactly a good spot for a honeymoon."

All right, so Arik was playing mind games, she thought. They might be in a bad situation here. Dinah smiled. "Is it safe for me to go outside and stretch my legs a bit?" she asked as graciously as she could.

"Sure," Arik said and gently took her hands to lead her outside. Arik gestured at the building that looked like a bunker and the endless, rolling black hills beyond. "What a future we have here!" He grinned at Dinah.

She said nothing but glanced at Grace and the guard standing behind them. If she had Madeline's psychic ability, she could have channeled into Arik's mind to communicate. But not only did she and Arik not have that ability, they also disagreed in every second conversation they had.

There was no chance for psychic communication with Arik.

Dinah approached him, and she tiptoed and kissed him.

He immediately responded. When their faces were close, she asked, "What's happening?"

"I think they're robots. When they captured us, the one that looks like Grace didn't recognize me."

They kissed, and whispered, then kissed again.

"Who did you tell them we are?"

Arik glanced at the robots. "I told them we work for Arete. We're married and on our honeymoon. I couldn't believe they believed that crap."

"What crap? The lie or the pretend marriage?" She bit lightly on his bottom lip.

He retracted his lip slightly to avoid another encounter with her teeth. "The lie, of course. Why do you always have to take what I said the wrong way, Dinah?"

"All right, so they're robots. I recognize their behavior. They're clones and very low-tech. Between the two of us, we can easily take them out."

"Yes, but the tracker led us here for the Yellow Shield tribe. The robots might know something."

Dinah nodded. "All right, let me handle this."

"Are you sure? I don't know who their master is. We say one wrong thing to them, and our honeymoon will end in a bloodbath."

"Arik, I might not always say the right thing. But I'm sure I can press the right buttons in these robots. They need to be reprogrammed."

She kissed him deeper, and her hands roamed his back.

His voice muffled by her kisses, he said, "If you keep doing this, I can't be held accountable for how my body reacts."

"Well, show me!" She glanced at the robots. They stood watching them. She kissed Arik harder, pushing him back and against the wall of the bunker. She could tell he was a little breathless and was holding back with all the willpower he had.

She slid her hands under his shirt.

"Dinah..."

But she didn't let him talk. She kissed him again then nibbled lightly at his neck and slid her hands into his pants.

He threw his head back, and it hit the wall as he let out a moan.

From the corner of her eye, she could see the two robots turn. Their backs were now facing them. As fast as lightning, she rushed at them. She used both hands to slam at the critical circuit point at the base of their necks.

The robots stood frozen. Now she could open them up and reprogram them to take Arik and her to the Yellow Shield tribe. Not hearing anything from Arik, she turned around and saw him standing, glaring at her.

"I manipulated your sexual urges. I'm sorry."

"You're *sorry?*"

"Yes. I'm sorry you're sentimental about this, but we did more than just kiss before—and you were fine, or appeared to be fine."

"My feelings don't matter to you. You were wrong to do that."

"These robots wouldn't take my commands, and we couldn't attack them head on without triggering some kind of alarm. I needed them to turn around and expose their weak points to me. Humans emit sex scent signals in the form of pheromones. All robot models can read that signal. They're programmed with a social etiquette function to respect others' privacy—"

"Dinah, I don't care." He walked back into the bunker and slammed the door.

CHAPTER 25

Cooper looked at Asana with disdain.

"I respect the elderly, Asana. But my patience has a limit."

"You're so patient that you left the house, knowing any movement you make will spread the poison further," Asana said in English and then chuckled.

"Oh, so you do speak English. That makes the fact that you pretended to be a harmless old man even more pathetic," Jenny said.

"I can't let you leave, Cooper."

"I wouldn't think so. You want my Iilos wrist unit. I mean, you want a function in it." He raised his hand as if he was going to press a button on it.

"No!"

Cooper smiled. "You're quite knowledgeable, Asana. You want the UAS, don't you?" Then he turned toward Jenny. "It's the Ultimate Asylum Status to the Daimon Gate. It's designed for Iilos privileged citizens. If you activate it, it will give you unconditional protection by the Daimon Gate."

Asana growled, his eyes glued to Cooper's wrist unit.

"I don't know what your plan is. But eyeing the UAS, you must have planned some serious shit at the multiversal level and prepared for the worst." He had a feeling that if he swung his arm in rhythm, Asana's would have danced.

"If you give it to him, he'll kill you, Cooper."

"He's already killed me, Jenny."

"There's an antidote," Asana said.

"Now we're talking," Cooper said. "So you want to trade the antidote for the UAS, right?"

Asana nodded.

"All right, give me the antidote. If it works, I'll give you the UAS."

From his pocket, Asana pulled out a tube of blue liquid.

"How do I know you won't poison me for the second time?"

"You don't. You'll just have to take my word for it."

Cooper shrugged. "My chances of surviving the poison are slim, but I still trust those odds over your ability to keep your word. Why don't you drink half the liquid, and I'll drink half? That will at least allow me to last a bit longer. Then we'll go back to your place where you can give me the rest of the antidote. If it is really a cure, it won't kill you."

"Poison treats poison. That's the way wolfsbane works. I don't have the poison in me. Taking the antidote will kill me."

Cooper chuckled. "Well, then there' appears to be no solution. I'll die with the UAS then."

Asana's face turned red as he tried to control his temper. Before he could say anything, as fast as lightning, Jenny pulled out the knife from Cooper's pocket. Asana was distracted by the unfinished deal and didn't react fast enough. Jenny slashed the knife across his chest. Asana jerked back, but the knife had cut into his flesh.

Asana lost his balance. Jenny gave him a hard kick. He reeled backward and fell over the lip of the well. Jenny dove over to grab the antidote tube, but she was too slow.

Asana gripped the tube in one hand and the edge of the well with the other.

"Give me the tube. If Cooper takes it and is fine, I'll pull you up." She stabbed the knife into the hand that gripped the mouth of the well.

Asana roared and let go. Jenny grabbed his hand.

Asana dangled over the maw of the well, held up only by Jenny's hand. "Give me the tube, and I'll pull you up."

He smirked at her. He held up the tube. "Poor judgment, Cooper. This is the real antidote. You've lost your chance." He yanked his hand out of Jenny's and fell to the bottom of the well.

Cooper slumped to the ground. Jenny rushed over. "Don't you die on me, Cooper. We're so close to the border. If you use your UAS, would they save you? Give you medical assistance or something like that?"

"No, you take the pass and go, Jenny. It's transferable..."

"Open your eyes. Look at me!"

He could feel her dragging him across the ground. Then his world went black.

CHAPTER 26

Arik followed the robot that looked like Grace and the guard into a dark tunnel. Dinah was right beside him, but it seemed like there were mountains between them. She had reprogrammed the robots, and now they were leading them to where they could find the Yellow Shield tribe. If technology came to Dinah so easily, why was she having trouble understanding that human emotion and sexuality were not robotic functions that she could manipulate at will?

Arik pointed at the robots. "Can we talk while they're here?"

She nodded. "I disabled all their programs. They only have one mission left, and that is to take us to your people."

"The Yellow Shield tribe aren't my people. I owe them."

She shrugged and said nothing.

A small group of humanlike creatures exited from a side of the corridor as they approached. Grace and the guard pulled their weapons, some sort of powered swords. Before other the creatures could react, their bodies copped slashes. Turned into piles of scrap metal, they convulsed on the floor, melted, and evaporated into thin air.

"I forgot to tell you, I entered a new command so they will protect us." She walked on before Arik had a chance to respond.

They reached the end of the corridor and approached a solid, black wooden door. Grace tapped it. A small window opened from the inside, and a pair of eyes stared out. Before any conversation could begin, the guard pierced the head of the creature inside with his sword.

"Did you turn them into mercenaries?" Arik asked in astonishment.

"No, their command is to protect us. They'll do whatever it takes to accomplish the task."

"It was just a rhetorical question."

She turned and looked at him. "And that was a rhetorical answer."

They turned to another connected room. The creatures in that room weren't expecting visitors. As they had before, the two robots charged at those in the room. The creatures dropped to the ground, wriggling in pain before they died, and their bodies severed metal bodies soon evaporated into thin air.

Next, they stopped in front of a giant steel door. Grace flipped opened a rusty box and punched in a code. The door lock clicked open.

Grace and the guard turned around, looking at Dinah. "Mission accomplished," they chorused. Then their heads exploded, and their bodies melted and evaporated.

Arik, startled, jumped aside. Dinah cast him a glance then proceeded to the door and pushed it open.

Inside, the bunker was silent. It was as eerie as the atmosphere of a tomb.

There must have been more than two hundred people in that cold, square bunker. Dim, flickering lighting. Poor ventilation. They stood up, watching as Arik and Dinah stepped inside. Hundreds of pairs of eyes. Sad, hollow eyes.

Arik's heart skipped a beat. If they were indeed his people, he had abandoned them. It was his fault they were in this condition.

"Arik?" a woman's voice called out, sending a chill up his spine. It was a haunting cry from his past.

The crowd split. From its midst, a beautiful woman with a hauntingly sad face walked out.

"Xanthe?" Arik felt a lump in his throat. The beautiful healer of the Yellow Shield tribe now looked like a ghost, frail and sad. Was he responsible for this?

Tears streamed down Xanthe's face. She turned around and spoke several sentences in Xiilok that he couldn't understand. But in front of him was unmistakably the village of the Yellow Shield tribe—one that had saved him and nurtured him back to life.

Xanthe approached him, her body shaking with emotion. "I knew you'd come back for us." She looked at Dinah. "Lamixg said you were going to come back and save us." Several people standing in the back burst into tears.

"Lamixg means leader in their language. Xanthe is the healer of the village," he translated to Dinah.

But he could see that she had turned on the translator in her wrist unit and could understand perfectly what was being said.

He could see tears gleaming in Dinah's eyes. Perhaps there was human emotion in her after all. He turned toward Xanthe. "I'm here to take you home. Where's Lamixg? He said I didn't have to start my leadership until he completed what he needed to do."

Xanthe nodded and gestured the way. They followed her toward the back of the basement. She pushed open another set of doors. Chill air blasted out, mixed with the scent of death.

Inside the dark room were rows and rows of corpses.

Arik froze at the door, unable to move his body. Xanthe tugged at his elbow. He nodded and followed her in.

In the corner, the man with the yellow-shaded eyes, the leader of the tribe, the one who had picked him up from the black mud where he lay waiting to die and had taken him back to safety, lay dead and frozen. Was this his fault for denying his responsibility for years?

"How did he die?" he asked although he didn't want to know the answer. There was nothing he could do to change this.

"He came back to tell us you accepted the position and were coming back to take us to a safer place. He had some other arrangements with the Eudaizian. But that night, Grace came with a man. They were chased, and we helped them. But then the whole village was swamped with the Red Shield. They captured us and killed Lamixg and your wife."

Dinah's eyebrow shot up, but she instantly neutralized her expression and looked away.

Arik nodded. At Carfax Tower, Grace had escaped with a man and left a space creature in disguise in the tower with him. It made perfect sense—she had run back to the Yellow Shield tribe to seek shelter. But she had taken a stranger and deadly enemies back to the tribe.

Arik sighed. *I'm so sorry,* he thought. *That's my fault.* He turned to Xanthe. "Do you know the way out of here?"

"Yes, we need only to cross over the hill. But this place is surrounded by dead swamps. The only way out is to fight through the Red Shield camp. There are only women and children here. There is no way they can survive either the swamps or the fight."

"Where are the men?"

"Most of them were killed during the attack. We were not equipped for combat."

Arik nodded.

Xanthe continued, "Some of the survivors have regrouped on the other side of the hill. They wanted to rescue us, but Lamixg asked them not to. He knew it would be another bloodbath, and they would lose. He asked us to wait here for you, and for the men to wait on the other side of the hill."

"How could he be so sure?"

"He had a vision before he died." Xanthe looked into his eyes. "He saw you save us as an angel."

"I'm no angel, Xanthe. But I'll do my best to get people out of there." As he turned around, he saw a tiny body lying on a bench at the far end of the room. He froze and then started to walk toward the body.

Xanthe pulled at his elbow. "Don't Arik. We've lost Liv, but we still have the other five children. If you don't get them out now, we'll lose all of them."

He nodded. "I need a moment to talk to Dinah."

Xanthe nodded and backed away.

He led Dinah outside the room. He braced his hands on the wall, closed his eyes, and inhaled deeply. He pounded his head against the stone wall. The image of Liv flashed back to him, plaguing his mind.

He had been recovering in Xanthe's healing chamber. Liv came every day. She brought him water and wildflowers she had picked herself. She was the size of a toddler but had the mind of a five-year-old. She was gifted with healing power.

Now she was dead, and he was staring at a wall. He felt Dinah's hand on his shoulder and shrugged it off. He didn't mean to. But he did.

"I'm going to take them home."

"As an angel? Because you need miracles to do that. We've only dealt with two robots and had so much trouble already. We can't use guns in Xiilok. And this place is surrounded by dead swamps."

"I have a solution. But I'm going to do it on my own."

"So you don't need me?"

"No."

She looked up and him and said, "Okay, fine." Then she turned on her heel and walked away.

CHAPTER 27

Cooper opened his eyes groggily and saw Jenny's bright face looking at him.

"There you are." She smiled at him then turned to talk to someone. "Can he sit up now?"

He blinked to clear his vision and saw a man in a white coat looking down at him. He sat up.

"You're a lucky man, Cooper Donovan."

He looked at Jenny and then back at the man. "Yes, I am. Who are you?"

"I'm one of the gatekeepers at the Daimon Gate. Ms. Bonneville..."

"Jenny."

"Jenny ran over to the gate with the Ultimate Asylum Status. She used that to ask us to help you. Normally, it wouldn't work. And what you needed was medical help, not protection. But because you are Eudaizian—"

"Am I?"

"Yes, we scanned your unit."

"I gave them the phone Ciaran gave you." Jenny grinned.

"And you do have a pre-registered privilege, an agreement between Eudaiz and the Daimon Gate. Therefore, you'll have all the medical assistance you need. The poison in you is mostly treated—"

"Mostly? So I'm only half alive?"

The man smiled. "No, you're a hundred percent alive in this dimension because we have corrected the corrupted blood cells and everything the toxin damaged in your body. There are, however, some otherworldly elements that our technology couldn't handle. So if you travel to another dimension within the material world, or if you cross worlds, you must be careful."

***

From the top of the middle hill, looking at the hillside outside the bunker where the Yellow Shield tribe was held captive, Dinah watched Arik from a distance. She knew what he planned to do now.

The middle hill looked down on the bunker, and she could see the hill the tribe members had to cross to get back to where their men were waiting. She had seen Arik do something similar when he'd formed the light bridge from hilltop to hilltop for Ciaran. But when he'd done it that time, he'd had help from Jael, the angel of light.

Now he was alone. He had formed a bridge by himself when she was injured, and Ciaran needed to carry her back to safety. But Ciaran said it had taken a toll on him.

And that bridge had been for only two people.

This one would be for more than two hundred people of the village tribe. She didn't know how he could do this. But those women and children seemed to hold a very special place in his heart, and he would do whatever it took to bring them home.

Arik had told her Jael had shown him something he could use. She didn't know what it was. But she knew Arik was no angel.

He walked around the top of the hill. The ground was covered in rocks and meteorites in many different shapes, sizes, and colors. He stood in front of a few large, shiny rocks that arched above him, looking like giant gates. He braced his hands on the two sides of the rock arch, and he looked up.

She smiled. He was smart.

This spot was the ideal position for solar attraction, the sort of light shining on this universe in its own cycle. In the material world, they had the solar system. People on Earth had the sun. But Xiilok was located in a universe in between.

This was a different kind of solar energy. It must be what Jael had taught him to use.

Arik glanced down to the valley and saw the village people standing outside their camp, waiting.

He closed his eyes and tightened his grip on the stone arch.

Dinah saw sparks above and heard the rumbling and crackling sound of a large amount of solar energy being drawn. The light shone down to the arch, and Arik bridged the light from the camp to the other side of the hill. The bridge was magnificent, as big as the hill itself.

Xanthe stood in front of the crowd. She led, followed by her five children, as beautiful as little angels. They walked quickly onto the bridge.

But the rest of the village people hesitated.

"Come on!" Dinah muttered. She understood why they would be scared. After all, the light bridge had appeared right in front of them.

Xanthe and the children set an example for the rest. They moved farther onto the bridge and waved their hands to encourage the others to come.

Arik opened his eyes and looked down the valley at Xanthe. Dinah knew with the brightness of the light, he wouldn't be able to see her now standing at the side of the bridge. Judging by the look on his face, she thought he must feel the weight of the people moved across the bridge of light.

"Come on, move!" she said again. But it didn't help.

A small stream of blood trickled from Arik's nose.

It was not just the weight of people, but also holding the light together. It must have been taking a lot from him. He didn't look like he could hold it for much longer.

"Come on, walk!" she shouted.

Arik saw her now. He looked at her. The energy had been drained from him, and she could see the intensity of the light wavering. The bridge shook a bit, causing Xanthe and the children to reel.

That won't help, she thought.

Arik couldn't even speak. He held tight to the stone arch, but if these people didn't walk soon, his knees would buckle, and he'd have to let go.

How did she understand him so well? She could even feel his energy level. She felt the surge of energy within her own body.

She felt a connection to him.

She walked over and stood behind him. She wrapped her arms around his waist. With the halo of light around them, she knew the people looking up from the bottom of the hill wouldn't see the shadow of her tiny body. She spread her weaponry wings. Arik would look like an angel with his wings spread wide and a glorious light surrounding him.

Some people in the crowd burst into tears, and all of them started walking over the bridge.

She could feel him grunting with the heavy weight. His energy was dissipating at an alarming level.

Dinah touched the mark of the jumper at the back of her neck. Perhaps she was destined to do this. There wasn't time to think about it. She pulled out her needle stack and opened a compartment containing a needle with a red tail.

She pulled it out and jabbed it into the mark at the back of her neck, the round circle marking all individuals who had jumped over the aperture of the multiverse—a rare event that bore a reputation for accentuating individual natural talent and bringing power.

She hadn't had any special power her whole life. At least that was the story she had told others, and it was true. What she hadn't told anyone was that she knew how to trigger the effect, even if it didn't happen naturally.

She felt the pull of energy instantly. And she knew what she had to do.

She yanked Arik's shirt off and saw a glowing spot on his spine below his neck. She drew solar energy into her body, poked a large needle into the glowing spot on his back, and transferred her energy to him.

In a short moment, their energy was connected, as were their bodies and souls.

***

Cooper looked up to the hill in front of him. "Bloody hell, that's Dinah and Arik."

Jenny turned around. In front of them, her brother and Dinah glowed in a magnificent wedge of light. They scrambled to their feet and ran in that direction.

CHAPTER 28

The bridge glowed brighter, and the people moved faster over it. Xanthe stopped near the end of the bridge to ensure everyone had crossed over. She looked at Arik, bowed with appreciation, and left the bridge.

Arik withdrew the bridge. She wasn't sure if he was even aware of what he was doing now. His head lolled back, and he collapsed onto her. She lowered him to the ground.

"Arik, open your eyes. Talk to me, please."

He was totally out of it.

Then Dinah felt the ground shaking. She looked behind her and saw the giant head of Roallix slowly emerging from the other side of the hill. Then his body. He opened his mouth to smile, and she could feel the heat waves coming out from between the sharp pieces of ivory rock that served as his teeth.

She pulled Arik backward and tucked him behind a rock. Then she charged at Roallix's face, pumping out her most lethal needles. She wasn't surprised to find they caused no damage.

She pulled out her gun and fired. The laser beams erupted from the gun, went sideways, and hit a large rock, sending it collapsing to the ground.

"Oh, that's totally unfair! Look at the size of you compared to the woman you're fighting!" Cooper shouted, charging up from behind her, followed by Jenny.

"Can you two take Arik and go? He's behind the rock." She pointed at Roallix, who was either smiling evilly or grinding his teeth. "This thing doesn't understand reason."

***

Arik opened his eyes. He could hear the commotion but couldn't see anyone. He was tucked between two large rocks. *Dinah*. The memory rushed back to him. He tried to sit up, but every movement was like trying to move a mountain.

Then Jenny rushed over. "Thank god you're okay." She reached down to give him a hand. He grabbed her hands so she could help haul him up.

"What's happening?"

"Dinah and Cooper are fighting a hulk."

The world in front of him was a blur. "No, I can't move yet. I'll only be a burden. Go help them." He leaned against a rock.

"All right. You stay right here, Arik."

Jenny left him and rushed back out.

Arik bore his weight on the rock and worked his way slowly around and out to the front.

There he saw the giant he thought they had killed before. It roared at Dinah. She had stabbed her knife to its face, and it had thrown her backward, sending her rolling across the rocky surface. Cooper pulled out his knife and was about to attack. Jenny came up from behind him. She picked up a rock, ran to get momentum, and threw it at the hulk's eye.

Bullseye. It roared again.

In front of Arik's eyes, the creature swung its gigantic arm like a crane and knocked Cooper and Jenny off the hilltop, tossing them like rag dolls to the mouth of the canyon.

From the ground, Dinah shot up, wings spread. She flew down to the canyon to save Cooper and Jenny.

Roallix bent down. He grabbed Dinah by the wings and pulled her up. She wriggled in his grip like a desperate little bird. He held her wings and smashed her body to the ground, over and over again.

Arik pulled out his gun. He knew shooting here wouldn't work, but he had to try. He tried doing what he saw Ciaran do with the sword. He used whatever strength was left in his body to concentrate his light energy into the gun, and he pulled the trigger.

Instead of the normal laser beam, a wave of light came out and hit Roallix right in the middle of the head. The beam immobilized him, and he dropped Dinah, but not before tearing off her wings.

Arik slumped to the ground. He knew he had nothing left. He couldn't move. He lay down and waited for Roallix to come and savage him.

The hulk stomped his feet in anger and moved toward him. And then he saw Dinah surge up from the ground.

No, it wasn't her. It was something else.

Her porcelain skin glowed in a halo of white light. Her eyes were bloodshot. Her long raven hair had turned as white as a cloud. And her tiny body floated, hovering above the ground.

Roallix was stunned. He paused and stared at the tiny white person floating in front of him.

"A life for a life. A heart for a heart. Magic for magic. A curse for a curse. I swear to my god, whoever kills me has to die the same way I did. In any world, at any time, that devil cannot return to life," Dinah said and raised her arms, pointing toward Roallix as she spoke.

Roallix frowned.

Then her tiny arms stretched out as fast as lightning. Before Roallix could do anything, she ripped his heart out.

He looked down at the hole in his chest, and the heart dripping blood in front of him.

His heart evaporated into thin air. And then so did his body.

Dinah's body flopped to the ground.

Arik crawled toward her and pulled her into his arms. There was nothing left in her. Not even a pulse. But this was Dinah, the person—or the alien—he had known. Her skin and her face had returned to normal.

But her hair remained white.

He heard the sound of wings flapping, the sound of something landing, and then footsteps behind him. But he was beyond care. There was no way his sister and Cooper had survived that fall. And he didn't know if Dinah could be revived.

Jael stepped out in front of him. He reached out for Dinah. Arik clutched her tighter in his arms.

Jael grabbed them both. Then it seemed as if they were flying. Everything around him turned white.

He heard Jael's voice say, "You're destined to be together, Arik. Treasure her."

CHAPTER 29

Arik awoke on a comfortable feather bed. Xanthe smiled down at him.

"An angel brought you here."

He bolted upright. "Where's Dinah?"

"In the adjacent chamber."

He scrambled out of his bed and rushed toward the door.

He made his way into the chamber, pushing his way through many doors and dangling curtains.

There he found her, with a knife in her hand. She had cut off half of her long white hair.

"Hey, no, no, hold on." He tried to pry the knife from her hand.

"What is this?" she growled as she gestured at her white hair.

"You know how much it would cost to pay for this beautiful white hair? If you want a haircut, I'll take you to a hair salon, okay?"

Tears streamed down her face. "Something happened to me, Arik. I've turned into something else."

He put the knife away, looked her up and down, and turned her around. "Your limbs are the same, you have one head and no tail, and you're still short. Except for the white hair, I can't see anything different."

"There was blood all over my hands."

He pulled her into his arms and held her tightly. She resisted for a bit and then was still.

He tilted her chin up and looked into her dark eyes. "We fought a monster. Yes, something in you changed, and because of that, you killed Roallix. Otherwise, we would have died. You don't remember any of that?"

She shook her head, and a tear rolled down her pretty face. Then her eyebrows shot up. "Cooper and Jenny! Where are they?"

"Roallix threw them off the cliff."

"They're dead? Oh no, did they die?"

"Look at me, and you tell me if they died, Dinah."

She scrambled toward the pile of her belongings on the floor and pulled out a small device. "Silly Cooper, give me a signal." The device stared back at her, a blank screen. She waited. Arik sat down next to her and wrapped his arm around her shoulders.

Together, they waited.

One moment passed.

Then two.

Then some more.

Suddenly...a happy ping.

Dinah grabbed the machine. "A signal, a positive signal. This was triggered, not automatic. We can search for them using this."

She hurried to her feet.

Arik held her shoulders.

"It will keep. Cooper and Jenny are very capable. They can take care of each other. We need to talk."

"All right. What do you want to talk about?"

"You don't remember what happened on the hill?"

She shook her head. "It just felt wrong. I don't know what happened." A tear rolled down her face.

He wiped it away with his thumb. "It might be better that you don't remember."

"No, I want to know what happened. If you saw something, tell me, please."

"I fell."

"What?"

"I fell in love with the beautiful woman in front of me. Whether she's human or alien, I don't care. White hair or not, I don't care. I do care about the fact that you don't know how to love. But I'm going to fix that."

"But you're married."

He locked his lips with hers and could feel her body vibrating with emotion. When he finished with the kiss, he traced his finger along her jawline. "I'm not married to Grace if that's what you mean." He traced his lips down her neck. "I was discontented in my life. So when I figured out the aperture, I thought it was just lightning, and I jumped. Grace followed me. The Yellow Shield tribe picked us both up. Grace's dying wish was to be a perfect woman, and to be my wife. So that's what they made her."

He lifted her up, and her legs spontaneously wrapped around his waist. He carried her to the bed and put her down, placing her on her back. His hands roamed over her body, and she let out a little moan.

"You thought I was married, and yet you fought the monster in front of me. I asked you to go, but you protected me and helped those strangers...unconditionally. You're full of compassion, Dinah. More than any human I've known."

"Compassion is a—"

He locked his lips on hers to stop her from talking.

"Open your eyes. I want you to look at me," he said, and she obeyed. "*This* is lovemaking, Dinah. I want you to feel it the way I do. And I want you to see what I feel."

Then he penetrated her.

She grabbed the sheet, a sound of pleasure escaping her lips.

He looked into her eyes and brushed a stray white strand of hair off her forehead. "I don't care what you are or what you've become. I love you, Dinah Greenwoods."

He could see that what he said registered in her eyes. A tear rolled down her cheek. He kissed it off.

"Love is sacred, Dinah. Being able to love isn't a uniquely human ability. You can love more than anyone I know. You can feel it." He picked up her hand and placed it against his chest.

She traced her finger around the position of his heart. She felt the heartbeats. She smiled at him as another tear rolled down her face. "I love you, too, Arik."

"See, it's not that scary." He kissed her. And then they brought each other to the peak of pleasure.

***

Arik pushed his face into the soft feather blanket, searching for Dinah's skin. He couldn't find her. He sat up. It had gone dark outside. Her scent still hovered in the air, but her side of the bed had gone cold. He pulled the blanket away.

Blood.

Drops of blood left as a trail.

He scrambled off the bed.

On the floor, white feathers were scattered everywhere. They weren't feathers from a pillow or the blanket. These were huge feathers from the magnificent wings he had seen on Jael. These were feathers from angel's wings, pulled out at the skin, leaving traces of blood.

Dinah's clothes were on the floor. Her weapons were on the bedside table. Her needle pack—the one she would never leave home without—lay next to her weapon, accusing him of letting something horrible happen to her.

He darted outside the chamber.

"Dinah!" he called out but was answered only by the darkness, the empty air, and the echo of his own voice.

CHAPTER 30

Arete didn't like the underworld much, regardless of how much potential its creatures had and the support they had promised him. But beggars couldn't be choosers. He could only do his best and play the game well as possible. But not everything was a game to him. Sometimes he did take things seriously. He just couldn't always recall when that was or what he took seriously.

Being immortal sucked.

The gothic door swung open. From a dark room inside came a stream of eerie white smoke, followed by a blast of cold air and then some soft footsteps. *Looks like a stage show of some kind. Should I be clapping?* he thought but then put that sarcastic stream of thought away.

A tall figure that looked like a skeleton with a small amount of loosely hanging flesh walked out. Arete shuffled through memories in his mind, trying to recall the name of the god he was about to talk to. When nothing came to mind, he gave up. He bowed respectfully and said nothing. It was a lot less risky to remain silent than to speak an incorrect name.

"I don't believe we've met," the skeleton man said.

"You previously dealt with a friend of mine—Asana."

"Oh, I remember him. Is he dead?"

"No, he had a little incident and couldn't come. He sent me instead."

The stick figure scratched his jaw with his bony fingers. "I didn't wish him to die, as he owed me so much."

"Whatever he owes you, I'll pay. But we need a little extra help."

"I'm not willing to invest any more."

"You would, if you'd hear me out. I know Asana had a deal with you to take out a human president of a country called the United States of America because he is opposed to the dark side of the magical world."

The skeleton chuckled. "You don't have to be polite. That president, whatever his name was—"

"Abraham Lincoln."

"Yes, whatever. He wanted to hunt vampires. He wanted to hunt my people. You see the problem? He's from the material world. We are from the magical world. We have nothing to do with his world. So why would he want to hunt us?"

"See, that's where you have it wrong."

"What?"

"With all due respect, you're wrong about the president. It wasn't him. It was his son, Robert Lincoln. You ordered Asana to possess one of the stage performers to kill Abraham. He was successful in this in the past. I, on the other hand, as a gesture of goodwill, manipulated one of my subjects to time travel there to stop the killing of the father and kill the son at the same time."

"I don't believe you'd do anything from goodwill. But let's say that was the case...then why are you here? As far as I'm concerned, Asana was successful. The father died. I couldn't care less what the son did."

"No, because Asana was successful, the son lived a full life and had a family. The child grew up to be the most lethal vampire hunter."

"Why should I believe you?"

"In my material world, there is a thing called technology. We can time travel to the past and future. I can simulate the future and see what the hunter will do to the vampires. Xiilok is an Amalgam world—I trust you know that. My friend in a tribe there can foresee the vampires' future, and it is consistent with the result from my time traveling simulations. If this isn't convincing enough for you, I can fetch you a crystal ball."

"So what's the solution?"

"We traveled to the past and tried to kill Robert Lincoln. Our attempt failed for unknown reasons. We burned that bridge, so that leaves us only one option—that I travel to the future and kill him for you. The hunter lives in the material world, so there is no other way to handle this."

"What's in it for you?"

"I really don't want to have to deal with this. But he lives in *my* material world, and he has messed up some of my business. I don't like that. Taking him out is going to be good for both you and me. I need someone to take care of the magical world."

"I don't believe you haven't placed a contact in my magical world who can do that work for you."

Arete chuckled. "Very good. You're cautious. The higher caliber entity I have in the magical world is Roallix, a dark angel. But he was killed for eternity."

The skeleton chuckled. "My condolences."

"No need to be polite. To kill the hunter in the material world, I need both the magical world and the Amalgam to be held steady. Someone has to be in control. Asana will handle the Amalgam. But you must help manage the magical world. Otherwise, there will be too many moving parts. And that's a formula for disaster."

The skeleton tapped his bony finger on the armrest of the chair, thinking. "All right, what exactly do you want me to do?"

"My major concern in the magical world is a couple—Jael and Charmine. They're angels, so you should be careful—"

"I'm not afraid of angels."

"Okay, all right. I need you to handle them. The best solution is to kill both of them. At the very least, one of them should be killed. I'd go for the wife. It will be easier to kill her than him."

"How long do I have to complete this task?"

Arete shrugged. "Well, it should be done as soon as possible."

The skeleton nodded.

Arete almost giggled on the way out. His largest problem had just been solved. He had no resources in the magical world. Now, with Roallix dead, it would be impossible to close the magical circle. Asana was right. Why not let the magical world circle sort themselves out?

Asana was now committed to Amalgam because he had been kicked down the well of second chance and hadn't been able to hold his breath long enough to not drink the water. He was now officially a Xiilok citizen. Asana didn't like the idea that he had no option. But Arete was pleased because he would never have to worry about Asana taking his part.

He shook his head and sighed. Partnering and teamwork had always been a challenge for him. He was a loner and had worked alone for a long as possible. But this circles business was too big to be a one-man job. He'd had to collaborate. The next thing he knew, he'd worked with Asana for centuries.

CHAPTER 31

Dinah looked down at her completely naked body. Then she looked up at the magnificent angel standing in front of her. She was standing in a round white stone room with arched stone windows.

"I don't feel comfortable in this outfit, or lack thereof."

"You should get used to it. You have a beautiful body. And you almost qualified as an angel."

"Jael, Arik told me you told him you're an angel."

"You don't seem to believe that."

"It's irrelevant. I didn't apply for an angel position. And I'm really not interested in that job. I work for Ciaran LeBlanc, in Eudaiz. Can I at least have something to cover myself? Even a bikini will do."

"You have your wings."

She chuckled. "Well, I used to. Roallix ripped them off. Now I have to crawl back to Ciaran and beg him to make me another wing suit. But it's okay—he can take it out of my salary. When he starts paying me of course."

"You're injured."

"Tell me about it. I have bruises everywhere. Before he tore off my wings, the beast held them and whacked me on the ground like I was a sack of potatoes. I killed him in self-defense."

"How did you kill him?"

"Weapons, of course. I don't really remember. I was totally out of it."

"You saw Ciaran kill Roallix with a king Sciphil sword. Roallix died but then came back to attack you. You killed him for eternity. How did you do that?"

"How do you know I killed him for eternity?"

"As I've said, I'm an angel. But not only that, I've never lost to anyone except for Roallix. I know how hard it is to kill him. And I would know if he is dead for good."

She nodded. Jael gave her a strapless white dress. She immediately slid it on. "Not exactly my choice of color, but it's better than nothing. Thank you. Why did you bring me here, at such an inconvenient time?"

Jael smiled. "By inconvenient, I take it you mean your intimate moment with Arik. He's a very good man. I approve of him."

"Approve of him? Excuse me? I don't think you're in a position to approve of anything I do!"

"Dinah, do you remember what happened when you touched my wife, Charmine, on the hill?"

"Yes, it still hurts."

"That happened because you went against the laws of nature. No matter what world you live in, you can time travel, but you are not to contact yourself. You and the child inside my wife are one and the same. You were not supposed to make contact."

She stared at the magnificent angel in front of her.

He approached her and wiped a tear that had rolled down her face. "Don't cry, my child."

"We met in 1864, and my mom was pregnant with me? So how old am I?"

Jael shook his head. "Age in the multiverse and the cross worlds is complicated."

She nodded. "I know. How did I end up in Xiilok with my other parents? Am I an angel? What's happening now? Why didn't it happen before?"

Jael smiled. "You have so many questions I don't have the answers for, Dinah. What I *can* tell you is that your mother and I had just gotten married. She was pregnant with you. Because our love for each other was so pure and strong, that made you a child of virtue that all devils and angels hunted for."

She frowned. "I'm sure they didn't intend to bring me up as a righteous and beautiful angel."

"No, you were mostly wanted for sacrificial rituals of dark magic."

"Can't you at least sugarcoat it a bit?"

"You can handle the truth because you are like your mother. She was a very strong woman."

"Where is she now?"

Jael shook his head. "I don't know. Back then, when she had just given birth to you, she was captured by her own tribe. But I'll find her."

"She was kidnapped? I'm a very good investigator. I'll help you find her."

"No, I'll do it myself. The reason I'm here is because of you, and it's urgent. Your Aunt Luna was one of the devils that wanted you. Before she was killed, Luna placed a curse on you, and she mixed blood with your mother. We didn't know whether the curse had worked, or whether Luna would take you. But seeing how you killed Roallix, I can now confirm both."

"What? That I'm cursed *and* possessed?"

Jael nodded and sighed. "It was a cold-blooded, heartless devil that ripped out Roallix's heart. It wasn't you. But it's in you, and it's strong."

Dinah looked at her shaky hands and the strands of white hair left dangling on her shoulders. "Did Arik see me?"

"Yes."

"He saw me turn into a devil? He saw how I could tear his heart out if I wanted to? But he just told me he loves me!"

"Now you know he really means it. And you didn't turn into a devil. You're possessed by it. You turned into an angel. That's the part Arik hasn't seen. Spread your wings."

"I told you, Roallix has..." she trailed off. She looked at her bare shoulders and then spread her real angel wings. Two magnificent feathered wings expanded out from her shoulders.

Jael smiled and looked at her with pride. "Having the wings of angel doesn't make you one. You need to be accepted into the house of the Gods.

But I'd be willing to bet that, just like your mother, you wouldn't want to go there."

She grinned. He approached and kissed her forehead. "Now, go back to your man."

"How do I know I'm not going to hurt him?"

"You won't know until you master how to control the devil inside you. You jumped through the light. You triggered your angelic make and your devil possession at the same time. You can control both."

She nodded, but her mind was plagued with doubts. Jael took her hand and led her to the balcony. "Remember, you have our love and blessing. Your mother is a gypsy of the multiverse with a free spirit. Like her, you will be strong. You can control the devil."

He flipped her over the balcony. She spread her wings and flew to the horizon, back to where she knew Arik was waiting for her.

END OF WOLFSBANE – DARK SOLAR TRILOGY
– BOOK 2
CONTINUE >>>

DARK SOLAR TRILOGY
Available at all major stores
Links and information can be found at
http://dnleo.com

Book 1 - Oleander
Book 2 - Wolfsbane
Book 3 - Maikoa

**For a limited time, D.N. Leo gives away
Several e-books and audiobooks in the Multiverse
Collection**

VISIT THE WEBSITE AND CLAIM YOUR BOOKS
http://dnleo.com

**THANK YOU FOR READING!
D.N. LEO**

D.N. LEO 'S NOVELS
SERIES READING ORDER

http://dnleo.com

A SHADE OF MIND
The Journey from Earth to Eudaiz
Main Characters: Ciaran, Madeline, Tadgh, and Jo
(Recommended reading in order)
1-4 Random Psychic
2-4 Forever Mortal
3-4 Elusive Beings
4-4 Imperfect Divine

—

MINDSCAPE
Main characters:
Ciaran, Madeline, Tadgh, Jo, Kyle, Hoyt, Ayana, Pete,
Sizx, Lorcan, Orla
(Recommended reading in order within series, can be
read in ANY order in related to other series)

Queen's Gambit
Knight & Pawn
Lone Castle
Doubled Bishops
Dead Squares
King's Endgame

—

SPECTRUM OF LIES

Main characters: Lorcan, Orla, Roy and Mori
(Recommended reading in order)

1-4 White Curse - Negotiate Death
2-4 Blue Fox - Befriend a Rogue
3-4 Indigo Stone - Cheat a Sorcerer
4-4 Red Moon - Break a Curse

—

SILVER BLOOD

Main characters:
Ciaran, Madeline, Tadgh, Jo, Caedmon, Sedna, Roy,
Mori, Zach, Mya, Lorcan and Orla
This series can be read in ANY order within the series
and in related to other series.

Virgo
Libra
Scorpio

THE GOOD DEITY

Main characters:
Main characters: Mya Portman, Zach Flynn, Leon,
Kirra.
This series can be read in ANY order within the series
and in related to other series.
Almost Countable
Almost Sure
Almost Everywhere

DARK SOLAR
Main characters:
Main characters: Dinah, Arik, Ciaran and Madeline
Oleander
Wolfsbane
Maikoa

MINDSCAPE ONE

QUEEN'S GAMBIT
KNIGHT & PAWN

OUTLANDERS OF THE MULTIVERSE
COLLECTION

BY D.N. LEO

Narrative Land Publishing
Narrativeland.com

SAMPLE

QUEEN'S GAMBIT
CHAPTERS 1-5

CHAPTER 1

Did the gray, dull, and inanimate garden wall in front of her just shiver, sweat, and leak out tears of blood?

This was incredulous. She wasn't Alice in Wonderland. Madeline shook her head. It must be fatigue. She looked at the wall again.

Now, it stood still as any dull gray wall in any backyard. She sighed. It was fatigue.

A strange shade of gray light spread over a garden of plastic-looking trees. Her eyes shot to the sky and widened. She was looking at the magnificent sunset in Eudaiz, a universe far away from Earth.

She smiled.

After what felt like decades of bloodbath and battles, she had survived and come here. The sunset was comforting.

Madeline had read many science fiction novels, which at the moment served the sole purpose of preventing her from freaking out or making a complete idiot of herself.

Then she realized the sunset in front of her was artificial.

The smile left her face, giving way to a frown of anxiety at the daunting thought of an uncertain future.

A few months ago, she would have laughed at the idea that she would ever space travel. But this was worse. She hadn't just space-traveled to get here. She had traveled across dimensions of time and space and God-knows-whatever-else. The sort of travel that didn't allow her to use a map to track the routes, the kind where she didn't know where she had been or how long it had taken her.

In 2015, she had been an accomplished New York journalist. A few short months later, she'd discovered she was not Madeline Roux, but Madeline Kelley. She was only half human from her mother's side because her father was Eudaizian.

She'd met Ciaran in London and discovered that she could love a man like madness. Ciaran said they were soulmates. But his words were too polished for her. She preferred to say simply that they loved each other. She'd married him a few days ago—in whatever dimension existed between Earth and this place.

She was now Madeline LeBlanc, in whatever year it was in Eudaiz.

Eudaiz was a multi-billion citizen universe, governed by a council of nine Sciphils—a word that stood for Scientist Philosopher. There had been countless times Madeline rolled her eyes internally when she used the term.

In her lay English, she considered the council to be like royalty or a government of some kind. They controlled everything in Eudaiz. What intrigued her most was that the council members were mostly humans who'd come from Earth. A council of nine humans governing an immense universe of alien citizens was a concept she'd never have imagined in her wildest dreams.

The thing was, her grandfather had been Sciphil One. Before he died, he'd appointed her as his successor of the Sciphil One position because she was the last living member of her family. So she was due to take up that appointment in a few days and became Sciphil One. That had been quite a shock to her peaceful life on Earth.

Suddenly her vision wavered. The garden in front of her flickered. "Oh, no," she muttered and turned around to go inside. On Earth, she'd thought she was a pseudo psychic. But since reconnecting with her biological family and accepting this Sciphil One position, her psychic ability had become stronger.

She could see minds and track minds, and sometimes she could even read people's minds. The baggage that came along with that ability was that she had precognition—mostly in regards to negative incidents. They called that her talent. She called it a curse.

She didn't think she could make it back inside the house. It seemed as if the ground was moving under her feet.

On the wall at the other side of the garden, a blood-red text appeared: *ENNEAD WILL KILL YOU ALL.*

The garden bed was covered in blood and gore. Body parts littered the ground.

She wanted to run, but her feet were buried in what looked like bricks made of dried bones. She yanked at her feet but couldn't free them. She called out for Ciaran, but no sound escaped her mouth. The bones built themselves up quickly, now reaching up to her body.

She was suffocating in a tomb of bone.

CHAPTER 2

"**W**elcome home," Kyle Wolf muttered to himself.

Kyle drew in the purified air of Eudaiz to remind himself of what he had missed in his thirty-three years living in exile. He swore to his soul that he would make those responsible for his miseries pay. In this universe—or in the one that contained Earth—his soul was the only possession he was sure was not illusory.

He chuckled at his analogy. As a mind-bender, Kyle's strongest talent was the ability to make others hallucinate. He could control people's minds. And he enjoyed doing it, especially when he made people kill themselves.

The stench of fresh blood always gave him a shiver of pleasure.

Deep in his thought, he tripped on a tub of water. He stared at his reflection in the purified water someone had put out in front of their house to give blessings for the new king of Eudaiz. The face mirrored back at him was a face he hadn't dared to look at for a long time—scarred, wrinkled, and ancient.

He had once possessed the typical angelic, Eudaizian look—and he'd had an innocent Eudaizian mind to match.

Those precious days were long gone.

Eudaiz was a place of happiness where people lived in total contentment and excelled at their individual talents. Eudaizians looked like extraordinarily beautiful humans. People here were born beautiful and saw nothing but beauty in their lives. There was no concept of heaven or hell because those benchmarks just weren't needed. This universe offered its citizens a true happiness that no other universe could.

Kyle cursed to himself and glanced from a distance at the happy crowds preparing for the king's coronation. Only those like him who had visited other universes could understand and appreciate Eudaiz, just as only those who had been to hell would appreciate heaven.

Kyle knew the difference between heaven and hell all too well. Eudaiz was a heaven—a perfect world that had rejected him.

"That should be *my* coronation," Kyle mumbled.

Eudaiz's constitution stated that people deserved happiness when they used their excellence to contribute to virtuous acts. But no one had ever clearly defined what a virtuous act was, and more importantly, what it was not.

Kyle clenched his teeth, thinking of the LeBlancs again. His life's work was down the drain now.

Bran LeBlanc, the previous king of Eudaiz, had cut off his eudqi—the life force that gave him his good looks and invincible strength. And Ciaran LeBlanc. Even the sound of the name made him feel as if his head was going to explode. Ciaran had taken the king's sovereignty. And that would terminate Kyle's existence.

"No!" He couldn't let that happen. "Damn you all. I curse you all," he growled. He whirled around in anger. "Ennead will kill you all. I swear to the gods of darkness, I will make them pay. The ennead will kill them all . . ."

A Eudaizian man carrying a tub of purifying water stepped out from a house and ran straight into Kyle. Half of the water in the tub poured out onto Kyle. Putting the tub down, the man turned to check on him.

He caught Kyle's face and withdrew slightly. Then he spoke politely in Eudaizian, "I apologize."

Kyle smiled. He understood that no one in Eudaiz was as ugly as he now was. Of course, the man was shocked seeing his deformed face. Kyle answered in his native tongue. "It's not a problem. I'm on my way to the Sciphil zone. I shouldn't arrive like this." He pointed at a few leaves and flower petals still hanging from his clothes. "May I use your facility to wash up?"

"Oh, of course. You're from the Sciphil council. My house is your house." The man pushed the door open and invited Kyle in.

Kyle shook his head. Naive Eudaizians should die. Kyle followed the man in and closed the door behind him.

Sensing something unusual, the man turned around and looked at Kyle. Kyle savored the fear in the man's eyes and the pain in his voice when he ripped the man's heart out with his bare hand. Kyle wiped the blood from his hand on the man's clothes.

He moved to the window and peeked outside. The air was filled with the distant sounds of cheering, music, and laughter. The aroma of burnt incense and fresh flowers whirled in the air for a moment and was then whisked away by the wind.

"Long live the king!" he hummed the words in his throat and smirked.

CHAPTER 3

Ciaran searched the garden and found Madeline fainted on the ground. His wife scared the hell out of him sometimes. He could see nothing unusual in the garden. The plantation in the garden looked plastic, but having dealt with chemicals for such a long time, he recognized that the material was organic, just not of Earth.

He knew for sure that the dome above that looked like sky was artificial. Its purpose was to create an environment that a human body could tolerate. The air inside the dome was normal. There were no strange creatures here or anything in the garden that he could peg as a sign of danger. *So why had Madeline fainted?*

He looked back at the house. It was more like a grand mansion than a bunker or a stereotypical space residence. Ciaran smiled to himself. Bran was Irish. It was only natural he'd build such a house to live in.

Ciaran noticed an old robot standing at the corner of the garden and approached it. It hadn't been operated for a long time. If dust existed in Eudaiz, the machine must have gathered a lot of it. He activated the robot.

The machine came back to life. After humming for a second, it blinked and looked at Ciaran. At first, the monitor on its chest was blank. Then it seemed to reconnect to the current network, and it updated its system.

Text appeared on the monitor on the robot's chest. "Please verify your access."

Ciaran pressed his right palm to the control panel.

"Left palm please," the text stated.

Ciaran pressed his left palm to the control panel.

"Welcome to Sciphil Three's residence, Ciaran LeBlanc—king-to-be of Eudaiz," the robot verbalized.

"Is there a surveillance system in this garden? I need to know what happened here before I activated you," Ciaran said.

"Yes. The data is available in your control room," the robot said.

Ciaran nodded and turned to go to the house.

"Please accept my condolences about Bran's death. It was a great loss for Eudaiz," the robot said.

Ciaran paused and looked at the machine. "You are one smart robot."

"My name is Robert. I am the first-generation robot that could potentially handle data from the EYE."

Ciaran glanced around to ensure no one was close by. "I thought you were a garden robot."

"No. I am the central robot. 245.21YZ ago, Bran deactivated me here because he was in haste to leave for a mission."

"How long ago?" Ciaran asked, arching an eyebrow.

"My apologies. Converted into Earth time, it has been the equivalent of thirty-three years since he deactivated me."

"No one has reactivated you since then. How do you know your information is up-to-date?"

"Only a King Sciphil can activate me. You will be King Sciphil in twenty-eight days from now after your coronation. You will have access to the full data of the EYE. My system has been connected to the central databank. It is up-to-date."

Ciaran hissed audibly. He didn't know how much intelligence they had here. How much surveillance data would be available and to whom. Attempting to access the EYE system violated multiversal law and would result in a death penalty.

"We are not authorized to access data from the EYE system. I have no intention of building that databank. Neither did Bran," Ciaran stated as clearly as possible to the robot. He knew the message was being recorded.

"You do not have to worry about surveillance. No one in Eudaiz has the privilege to access King Sciphil's data in his private residence."

Ciaran smiled. *You're a robot. You're allowed to be naive*, he thought. "All right, Robert, how many others have lived in this residence?"

"Pierre LeBlanc until 1655. Aedan LeBlanc until 1755. Ealga LeBlanc until 1805. Malachi LeBlanc until 1976. Bran LeBlanc until 2015. Current owner, Ciaran LeBlanc," the robot narrated the information in a monotone voice.

But every word cut at him like a knife on bone. Generations of his family had been involved in this. And he hadn't known. His parents had worked their whole life to keep him out of it. To spare him the pain of power and responsibility to people he didn't know.

Ciaran LeBlanc, King of Eudaiz. Ciaran shook his head. He wasn't sure how long it would be before he got used to this life. A few months ago, he was a business man, running his family global pharmaceuticals empire out of his London headquarters.

Now he was here, working toward his kingship. There would be a lot to do before his coronation. If claiming the kingship of this universe was easy, there shouldn't have to be much bloodshed required.

He glanced around. Every brick in this place was soaked with the mystery of his family. The mysterious aura that had followed his family for generations. From Earth to the multiverse. Some people considered his family the most mysterious family on Earth.

Perhaps they were right.

He looked at his hands. There was blood on these hands. He'd killed to get here. But as Bran had said, it took a life to save a life. He didn't have to be a virtuous king—he only needed to be a just king.

But would he be capable of being a just king? What would it cost him to do the right thing for the citizens of this gigantic universe?

His emotions were his weakness. He was a human, not a robot. And when it came to his family, he would not compromise. Ever. He would do whatever it took to protect them. Everything else came second to that.

Family!

It dawned on him now why Madeline had fainted.

CHAPTER 4

Madeline was agitated. She needed to tell Ciaran about her precognition. But since Ciaran had found her in the garden, he and the others had made her lie down like a sick puppy. She protested. But then they'd taken a complicated-looking wristwatch off her, and the next thing she knew, she felt as weak as . . . a sick puppy.

At a corner of the room, Ayana Dee, Sciphil Two, and Pete Chandler, Sciphil Nine were talking. They had helped her and Ciaran a lot during the process of coming here. Ayana had been born in Eudaiz. She was as beautiful as an angel. Pete was a British man, recruited later in his life. He was like a kind uncle to Madeline.

Ciaran strode into the hall from a wing of connected corridors. His face was unfathomable—a typical Ciaran expression. He crouched next to her. "How are you feeling?" he asked.

"I'm perfectly fine. I'll feel better if they give me back that wrist unit."

Ciaran nodded toward Ayana, who was holding the wrist unit. She approached and gave the little machine back to Madeline. As soon as she put it on, waves of energy pumped into her body. She felt like a new person. She sat up, but she wasn't sure if she should tell Ciaran about the precognition in front of Ayana and Pete.

After all, she and Ciaran had just arrived in this universe. They didn't know who were friends and who were foes.

"I've taken a look around the residence. Everything looks fine. We can stay here. The top priority for us now is to plan Madeline's officiation as Sciphil One, am I right?" Ciaran asked.

Ayana answered, "Yes, indeed. It is important that she receives her full power in Tower One. Her succession had been authorized and lined up at the precise astronomical time, two days from now. If we fail to officiate her, the power of Tower One will fail—and so will Eudaiz."

"Understood," Ciaran said.

"Let me show you the map." Ayana turned on a floating screen, revealing a map of Eudaiz.

Eudaiz was organized in circles. The towers of power, clearly labeled, stood in a protected area. In the middle was Tower Three, the king tower. The other eight towers were located in a circle surrounding it. They looked like the eight petals of a sunflower.

Ayana pointed to the king tower and said, "This is the core of Eudaiz's power. It must be protected at all costs. The king has access to all towers. However, each Sciphil has access only to their own tower. So, Madeline, after officiation, you will have full access to Tower One. I have full access to Tower Two. And Pete has access to Tower Nine. Ciaran has access to all."

Madeline gestured widely. "So, given how important the towers are, security is critical. This universe has more than six hundred billion citizens. This must be a massive area. How can you guarantee security for the towers?"

Ayana smiled. "The tower zone is called the Sciphil zone. No citizens are allowed in there. The area is self-contained and quite small. The security of the Sciphil zone is strict and has never been breached in five hundred years. The towers have no entry point for anyone except the Sciphil of the tower and the king. Within each tower, there are nine round protective layers—they would spin and grind any unauthorized individuals into dust if they attempted to trespass."

Madeline nodded.

Pete pointed to a large circle which wrapping outside of the Sciphil zone. He said, "This is the Sciphil residential area. Each Sciphil has a residence, located as close to his or her respective tower as possible. We are here, at Sciphil Three residence." He pointed to a dotted line. "The internal capsule is strictly private and secure. It operates only for people with the right access. The capsule terminals are like subway systems in New York or London. So really, within the Sciphil zone and Sciphil residence areas, I wouldn't worry too much about security."

Ayana pointed to a larger circle outside the Sciphil residential area. "This is where the six hundred billion citizens live." The area took up a large area of the map. Ayana continued. "There are eight districts, located in circles in the outer ring here. Each Sciphil governs a district. No citizen has ever been allowed into the Sciphil zone."

"There are nine Sciphils and eight districts. Who doesn't have a district to govern?" Ciaran asked.

"You, Ciaran." Ayana smiled.

Pete laughed. "You have to manage all of the Sciphils and handle important matters such as protecting Eudaiz from our enemies. I think it's only fair to exempt you from the administrative duties of governing a district."

"From what I know, the Black Rock is our number one enemy. Is that information accurate?" Ciaran asked.

Pete shook his head. "No. It's speculative. That universe attacks us all the time because they don't have much energy or natural resources. Other universes may have attacked Eudaiz before, but not during the five hundred years' reign or our Sciphil council. There is no guarantee they won't attack us in the future."

"Have the Black Rock ever breached our security in the Sciphil zone?" Madeline asked.

"No," Ayana responded.

Ciaran nodded. "All right. It's been a long day. I think we should continue this discussion tomorrow."

"It feels as if a day here has fifty hours," Madeline said.

Pete smiled. "We don't use hours. A day here has nine units. Three for the morning, three for the afternoon, and three for the night. Each unit has one hundred slots. At the moment, it is the fiftieth slot of the night. The average person should have at least one unit of sleeping time a day."

Madeline rolled her eyes. Another set of rules and numbers to remember.

"Thank you, Pete. I'll be sure we get enough sleep." Ciaran smiled.

Pete nodded. "Especially you."

Ciaran arched an eyebrow.

Pete continued, "The battles you engaged in before arriving here have drained you of all of your natural energy. In Eudaiz, energy is everything. It's life. Eudqi is a special energy for Sciphils. It's like your blood. However, in your case, you won't receive full power until after your coronation. So right now, your energy is fragile and very temporary. Be sure you take advantage of the resting time so that your body can recharge what's used up during the day."

Ciaran raised a hand in frustration. "What you're saying is that, at the moment, I don't have the natural energy to operate my body. And I have to rely on the eudqi—like batteries?"

"Precisely," Pete smiled.

"So don't pick a fight," Madeline laughed.

"We'd better go to sleep now," Ciaran muttered.

"Not here, I hope," Ayana said.

"Why not?" Ciaran asked.

"This place has been vacant for more than thirty years. It can't be comfortable. Madeline has a fully operational Sciphil One residence. You both have full access," Ayana said.

"Yes, we'll go to Sciphil One residence later. But I'd like to have a bit of time here with Madeline, if we may," Ciaran said.

"It's only for one night. We can manage. If you could stop by again tomorrow and take us to Tower One, it would be greatly appreciated." Madeline smiled.

Ayana nodded. "Very well then. We will let you have some privacy. It's been a long day."

Ayana and Pete left the residence.

Madeline opened her mouth to tell Ciaran about what she had seen in the garden, but before she could say a word, Ciaran had locked his lips with hers. Whenever he engaged in such an intimate act, she was defenseless.

Suddenly, Ciaran glanced toward the side door. "Who's that?" he shouted and darted toward the door, weapon drawn.

CHAPTER 5

A short moment later, Ciaran came back in with a grin on his face and a remote control in his hand. "It was a flying surveillance camera. This entire place is serviced by robotic staff. No humans. You can do whatever you want here without anyone gawking . . ."

He continued to speak, but all she could focus on was her sinfully handsome husband. It didn't matter what he said now. He was safe and sound. That was all that mattered to her. She shuddered recalling the battles they had just been through to get to this universe.

She couldn't forget the warmth of his blood on her hands. She had been tormented by hopelessness when he was going down and she didn't know what to do.

But they had left those incidents in the past. And she hoped never to experience that feeling again.

She smiled at him when he said something about the use of technology. She really did mean to tell him about her precognition. But hell, her stomach quivered with lust every time he spoke. She could easily forget the universe and drown in the sight and sound of him.

She still didn't understand how he could possibly be hers. Called her biased, but her husband had to be the most gorgeous and intelligent man in the cosmos. Six foot three—or maybe even taller. His slender frame made his clothes or whatever he draped himself in look elegant. Beneath the material were the muscles that were disturbingly and distractingly beautiful.

His long, thick black hair almost touched his shoulders, framing the God-given face she loved. His intense gray eyes always seemed look straight into her soul. They twinkled when intrigued, and she loved it when they twinkled because of something she had said. His lips were made for kissing, and to that point, that was exactly what she wanted to do right now.

Ciaran paused at the expression on her face. Then he smiled, and his eyes twinkled. He approached the bench where she sat, brushed his thumb across the dimple on her left cheek.

"My first councillor, what's on your mind?" he asked and kissed her. Apparently, he didn't expect an answer.

As much as it embarrassed her, she couldn't help but let out an audible purr at his kiss and touches. The movement of his hands on her body was heavenly. He knew every curve on her body better than even she did, but he still traced them with his long fingers—those of an artist.

Perhaps he was an artist—an artist in lovemaking. He was so inventive that she couldn't keep up with him. Every time they made love, it was like the first time. But this was the first time they had been intimate in this strange universe.

She slid her hands underneath his shirt. He knew her body. She knew his. They gave. They took. They moved together in perfect rhythm. A brush of the lips. The heat of a tongue on bare skin. The pressure of fingertips on sensitive spots.

They knew it all.

They had done it all.

But each time, it was a new experience.

And they enjoyed it. Taking each other to the pinnacle of pleasure.

After a while, they lay still until she hopped up and propped herself up on her elbow, glancing around. "Where exactly *are* we?"

Ciaran chuckled. "I'd call this a broom closet. But with the lack of a broom or other cleaning tools, I'm guessing it's some kind of storage room. What it's storing, I have absolutely no idea."

He kissed her forehead and lifted her chin. "Why are you so reluctant to go to Sciphil One residence? It will be yours soon."

"I'm not staying with you? If my memory serves me correctly, I'm your wife—so I ought to be with you, staying here."

"In the broom closet?" he teased.

Madeline played with his hair. "Why are you so reluctant to stay *here?* It's yours now."

Ciaran fingered her dimple again and drew her into his arms. "I need more people around to take care of you." He kissed her cheek. "You're pregnant."

Madeline snorted. "If we keep up this broom closet activity, it will happen soon!"

"You're already carrying our twins, Madeline—a boy and a girl."

Madeline stared at her husband, speechless.

END OF SAMPLE CHAPTERS

MINDSCAPE ONE
THE MULTIVERSE COLLECTION

HTTP://DNLEO.COM

Thank you for reading.

If you enjoyed reading **Dark Solar - Book Two - Wolfsbane**, I would appreciate it if you would help others enjoy this book, too.

<u>Recommend it.</u> Please help other readers find this book by recommending it to friends, readers' groups and discussion boards.

<u>Review it.</u> Please tell other readers why you liked this book by reviewing it wherever you purchase it. A few sentences will make a significant difference to me. If you do write a review, please send me an email at info@dnleo.com so I can thank you with a personal email.

Connect with me online:

http://dnleo.com

COPYRIGHT

Dark Solar 2 - Wolfsbane
By D.N. Leo

www.ingramcontent.com/pod-product-compliance
Lightning Source LLC
Chambersburg PA
CBHW070847260626
47170CB00007B/2533